WAYS TO
DIE
IN GLASGOW

OTHER TITLES BY JAY STRINGER

JAY STRINGER

WAYS TO DIE IN GLASGOW

A Rumpus in Five Parts

Published by Thomas & Mercer, Seattle

www.apub.com

Amazon, the Amazon logo, and Thomas & Mercer are trademarks of Amazon.com, Inc., or its affiliates.

ISBN-13: 9781477830109
ISBN-10: 1477830103

Cover design by Lisa Horton

Library of Congress Control Number: 2014958625

Printed in the United States of America

PART ONE

'Dead people are rude like that.'

—*Lambert*

One
Mackie

I'm baw deep in Jenny Towler when they come looking for me. I don't hear it at first because Jenny's doing all that fake shouting she thinks turns me on, and there's guys in the other rooms getting the same doing. But then I hear people running up the stairs, and the back of my neck goes—does that tingling thing that always saves my arse—and I'm up and moving.

They barge in through the door, a bald man covered in tattoos and some skinny blond guy carrying a gun. You know you've pissed someone off when they send a gun.

Baldy tries first. He calls my name and steps forward, reaching for me. That's easy enough—he's unarmed and my blood is up. I grab his outstretched arm and haul him towards me, then hit him in the neck with my other hand, almost punching through him. I feel something pop, and he hits the floor with a gurgling sound. Fuck yeah. That's good.

I hear the roar in my ears, the one my doctor warns me about.

Bouncy.

Bouncy.

Then I think about the blond. I turn around as he raises the gun. This isn't one of those visits they want me to walk away from. I've got a few seconds before he pulls the trigger. It would take me *a few seconds* to get across to him; the maths don't look good. His hands rock as he squeezes the trigger a couple times, and things go into slo-mo. Jenny T screams, and the blond turns and shoots her first. Her brain sprays across me and onto the wall behind us. Jenny always gets in trouble when she's with me. This gives me time to move, but before I can do it, the bald guy grabs my leg. He's climbed to his knees, still gurgling, one hand covering his throat while the other has my ankle.

I kick him in the face, once, twice.

On the second he lets go and tries to block me with his hand. Fuck that—he's annoyed me now. I follow all the way through with a third kick, and his nose pops inwards. A fourth is even harder, and his eye socket wobbles a little more than it's supposed to. He stops moving, and his eyes go all glassy. I turn back to the blond with the gun, but he's already sidestepped Jenny T and he shoots me, for real, in the fucking leg.

I've never been shot before.

I don't think I like it.

My leg goes cold. I would have expected heat, but like I say, I'm new to this. I think I'm going to throw up. I hold it in for a second, looking tough, but then I bend over and heave, and Baldy gets a full coating of my lunch. Blondie steps in closer, maybe to laugh at the wounded naked man throwing up his guts like a little boy. But that's his last mistake. I lunge at him, yelling, lift him off his feet and throw him against the wall.

I grab the gun by the barrel and swing the butt into his face. It connects hard. He falls down and I turn the gun around, feeling the weight and the power of it.

'I liked Jenny'—I put the gun into his mouth—'I really fucking liked her.'

I squeeze the trigger and take the top of his head off. He looks like a tin of baked beans, waiting to spill. Normally I hate guns, but this is fun.

I try to steady myself, but my leg is still numb and the world is getting far away. A blackout's coming, and I can't let that happen. I press the warm tip of the gun into my own wound, and the pain shoots through the coldness, giving me the kick I need to stand up. I stumble out the door and down the stairs. I think people are there watching me; I see them a million miles away at the edge of my vision, guys who've been fucking in the other rooms.

To them this place is probably just a bit of fun, bang for your buck and all that.

But I went to school with Jenny T, and now I'm pissed off.

Gotta find out who wants me dead and why.

But first I've got this whole being shot thing to deal with. I push out through the front door and turn right. My Uncle Rab lives a mile away. Can I walk that far on this leg? One way to find out. Things keep getting blurry, and the world comes back to me in flashes. I'm lying in a doorway, trying to stand up again. Then I'm being licked in the face by a cat as I rest on the grass outside Ibrox Library. Then I'm banging on the doorway to Rab's building before I remember he keeps spare keys under a slab in the front yard, for the nights he gets pished and loses his own set.

I let meself in and turn his shower on. Reckon I should clean up.

The dog's asleep in the kitchen. Great guardian. Little black and tan boxer, built for fighting, but Rab's gone soft and spoiled him rotten, so now he runs around just like barrels don't. I fuss the wee man's head, then stumble into the bathroom. There's blood on my hands, and it smears all over the shower dials as I turn up the warm water.

Then I'm done.

Two

I wake up with something like a hangover. Then I remember that I'm not hung over, I'm dead.

Except I'm not.

I should be. I mean, I feel like I am. I've got a headache and I can barely move, and warm water is hitting me in the face. I try and climb out of the bath, but I don't have the energy. Red water is swilling down the drain. That's odd—why is the water red?

Oh yeah. Blood.

Oh yeah. I got shot.

I'm not a doctor. I did get a doctorate off the Internet, but it was a comedy one that came with a cuddly toy and a year's worth of coupons for the slots at Las Vegas. I check out my thigh. There's a hole in the front that looks like a large burst zit—nothing to worry about. Round at the back, though, is a hole big enough to stick my thumb into. I try it, just for a laugh.

I don't laugh.

I throw up.

Note to self: Don't do that again.

Okay, I'm not dead, so the bullet must have missed anything that would kill me. But my skin is kinda white, and I'm moving really slow. That can't be good. I know a girl who can fix me up, but I gotta get going. I drag myself up the side of the bath, then lower myself down to the bathroom floor. I look for my clothes but can't find them. I guess I forgot to get dressed again when Blondie was shooting me. Did I walk all the way here in the nip?

Jaysus.

Not again.

People round here have learnt to live with me, I guess. Or to run away.

I crawl out into the hallway and pull Rab's phone down off the table, then dial a number and explain my situation, polite like, with a minimum of swearing. My doctor agrees to come round and get me. I can't climb up to the door buzzer, but I can make it to the front window, so I drop the keys down into the yard so she'll be able to let herself in like I did.

Then I think, fuck it, this bit of floor looks nice.

Three

A scream wakes me up. Well, more of a yelp.

Then I realise it was mine.

I'm lying on my belly, and my doctor, Beth, is sitting on the floor beside me, cross-legged with my wounded thigh in her lap. She's got nice blond hair that falls across her face as she works, and her cheeks flush a little when she's worried. Beth worries a lot when she's with me. She's stitching the wound closed with a needle and thread.

And it hurts like buggery.

There's a cord wrapped around my thigh, tight.

'What's that?'

'Don't ask.'

'How's my leg look?'

'Don't ask.'

I sniff the air. 'Why does the place smell of bleach?'

She pauses longer this time, her eyes flicking to mine for a second before concentrating on my leg again. She brushes some of that nice blond hair out of her eyes. 'Don't ask.'

Great, she's in a mood.

Beth and me go back a few years. When I was locked up, she was the doc who came and tried to fix my brain. Talked to me about what I'd done and how I felt about it. Asked what I remembered. Uncle Rab never visited, but Beth would come and spend time with me. We got to talking about everything. Then she convinced the judge I should be allowed out on my own. I'm meant to have appointments with her every week, but sometimes I forget, and she never reports me.

I think she likes me.

I try and turn over, but she holds me in place, so I talk into the carpet. 'It's going to be okay, aye?'

'I'm not sure.'

'How no? You're a doctor.'

'Mackie, I'm your psychiatrist. All I know about bullet wounds is what I've seen in films.'

'They don't teach that stuff at head doctor school?'

'Of course not. Look'—she pats my bare ass and slides out from under me, showing that she's finished—'we should get you to a hospital.'

'No way.'

'Mack—'

'No way. Uh-uh. They have to report shite like this, and then I'll be back inside. And they'll see all the favours you been doing for me, and that one time you got me those—yeah, you know—and you'll lose your licence, aye?'

'You're blackmailing me?'

'No, I'm looking out for you. I like what we got together, this weird little thing, and I wouldn't want them to lock you up or nothing.'

I see her jaw move against her cheek, like she's biting down on something; then she puts her hands up in the air. 'Whatever. What happened, anyway?'

I roll over onto my back and haul myself up into a sitting position with my wounded leg stretched out in front of me like a dead weight. I pull at the cord cutting off the blood supply, but she puts her hand on mine and stops me. She brushes that hair away from her face again and then nods. 'Come on, what happened?'

'They shot me.' I try for the joke, but she doesn't laugh. I drop my voice and look at the floor for a minute. 'They killed Jenny, Beth. They killed Jenny T.'

She sits back down on her haunches and looks cut up. 'No, Mack. Nobody shot Jenny. We've talked about this.'

'Then who the hell was I shagging last night?'

She looks like she's going to carry on speaking, give me one of her speeches about the way I deal with loss or grief or some other shite, but she stops. She picks a small knife up off the floor next to us and works the blade under the cord around my thigh, avoiding cutting the skin that has swelled up around it.

'Ever had pins and needles?'

She smiles at me with that twinkle in her eye, then cuts the cord.

Fucking.

Hell.

I thought getting shot was painful. That was quick and merciful compared to what comes next. Fire races down my thigh, running up and down my leg. It eats away at both the entrance and exit wounds, and I can't help but let out a silly little yelp. The pain runs around my foot and eats at my toes, and my head starts to feel like it's wobbling.

Beth starts rubbing at my leg, at all the bits that are hurting, and talking about the blood supply and nerve endings. Then I remember that I'm naked and try to cover myself up before things get real embarrassing.

'Nothing I've not seen before,' she laughs, then stands up and fetches a vial of pills from her bag in the doorway. 'You didn't take your pills yesterday, did you?'

These English birds, they have some silly ideas.

'I hate them.'

'I know, but you need them.'

She hands a couple of pills to me, and I slip them into my mouth, beneath my tongue, then make a show of swallowing. She opens my mouth and waggles her finger for me to raise my tongue, then waggles it again for me to swallow the pills for real this time. I do. I sit and wait for things to get boring again.

Gotta fight it.

Gotta fight the pills.

Need to know who tried to kill me.

Need to know who killed Jenny T.

Beth then looks down at me kinda funny, something in her eyes. 'Did you do it, Mackie?'

'Do what?'

'You *know* what.' She bends down and whispers, *'The dog.'*

13

Four

Beth helps me to my feet and leads me out into the hallway.

What I hadn't noticed when I'd come in last night was that someone had ransacked the place. Mail is scattered across the floor. Rab's wallet is lying in the corner with its contents all out around it. The furniture is tipped on its side in the living room, and the bottoms have been slashed out as if someone was looking for a hiding place. Rab's keys are here, so he was too. And he wouldn't have left without them. He's not an idiot like me. Someone came here and took him. Why would someone be after both of us? The only things we have in common are blood and our amazing singing voices.

Then Beth leads me into the kitchen and what's left of my wee heart breaks.

The fuckers killed Rab's dog.

Beth has cleaned up the mess, which is why I could smell bleach, but has left the wee man lying on top of a bin bag. He looks peaceful. His head is a mess, and it looks a lot like the wound in my leg. I guess he was a good guardian after all, tried to stick up for his old man and the bastards shut him up.

I ruffle the hair on his head again.

Now I'm fucked off.

Shoot me? Aye. I'm an annoying shite—I get that.

Shoot Jenny T to get to me? Well, she chose to be with me, I guess; she took her chances.

Grab my Uncle Rab? Well, Rab's pissed off a lot of people.

But shoot a dog?

I'm going to fuck them up big.

Then I remember something. 'Wait.' I turn to Beth. 'You think I'd do this?'

She looks nervous, like she knows she's wrong to doubt me.

'Well, you know, Mack, after that conversation we had yesterday, after some of the things you said, I don't know. I thought maybe—'

'What conversation?'

'You don't remember?'

Is she having me on? I stare at her, and she blinks back at me a few times. No. She's being serious. I don't remember talking to her yesterday, but then I don't remember much of anything other than being shot. I'm good at forgetting things, have been ever since they sent me down to the jail. And if I've been drinking—well, that makes it easier. Most of yesterday is a big black hole.

'What did I say?'

'I'll tell you later,' she says. 'First, let's get this mess sorted.'

We find me some clothes out of Rab's closet, a shitty cheap-looking trackie that he probably uses when he pretends to go running. Then we turn to housework. Don't want any signs of this mess if the cops come round; they would get in the way of what I need to do. Beth helps me put the furniture back where it should be, and when it's the right way up, you can't see the ripping. We clean the hallway and the bathroom, and then bundle up the wee man with a few of his toys. I help myself to Rab's wallet and a knife from the kitchen.

He won't mind.

We pack our bundles into the back seat of Beth's car, a small little French thing that's meant to be eco-friendly, and she looks over the roof at me before we climb into the front.

'You're not going to do something stupid, are you?'

'Course not, hen.'

Stupid? No.

I'm gonna kill a bunch of shitey bastards to avenge a hooker and a dog.

If that's stupid, then call me Elmer Fucking Fudd.

Five
Sam

I was woken by the phone ringing. I lay and listened to it, waiting for the machine to kick in.

Yes, I still had one. It had been my father's and was one of the few things I'd managed to retrieve from our old office when the bailiffs came in. It was twenty years old. I'd had to buy an adaptor to make it work with a modern phone. I'd thought about recording a new message when I took over the business, but people seemed to expect a male voice when they called a private investigator. It was still loaded with my father's old Rockford special: 'Ireland Investigations. Leave your name and number, we'll get back to you.'

I reached for my pack of emergency cigarettes but saw it empty and crushed into a ball on the floor. I only remembered smoking two of them the night before, but I also only remembered drinking one bottle of wine, and my head told me there had been more than that. I opened the drawer and found my electronic cigarette and sucked down the vapour, pretending it was the same. Sometimes you can sense a shitty day is on the way. I liked to give them levels—scores out of ten. The game was to guess at the start what level of shite the day would achieve. I'd got pretty good at it. I judged I was at the beginning of a seven. Maybe I'd be able to get it down to a six if I went for a run later, got some air into my brain and cleared out the booze.

I usually went for a run every day, but I'd been skipping it for a week, and already I was feeling the guilt, imagining the fat cells in my body taking hold. I ignored the phone. I'd had a lot of calls from journalists over the past couple of months and had got used to blanking them. I lay back and stared at the ceiling, but when the message started to record, I heard an educated voice. An east coast accent that carried the fake hint of Englishness you could only get from expensive Edinburgh schools.

I heard the name of a law firm and the start of a phone number.

I heard money.

Money would be good for the rent.

I fell out of bed and made it to the phone before the woman on the other end had finished. She paused for a moment when I picked up, and a little doubt crept into her manicured voice. I probably sounded like hell. I certainly didn't sound like someone who should be taking calls from her kind of law firm. She asked again if she'd called the offices of Ireland Investigations, and I said yes. I didn't tell her that she'd also called the bedroom.

She asked me to attend a meeting with her employer at 11.23 a.m.

I got a kick out of the precision in that request, and decided to show up at 11.25.

The name of the firm was Hunter & Simpson. I lied and told her I'd heard of them and that I didn't need the address. My father had taught me long ago, always pretend you've heard of someone if they have money. Always pretend you're on their level and that they should be paying you for things. He was better at pretending than me. He wasn't the one who'd lost the office. It wouldn't be difficult to find the address. They'd be online, or in the phonebook. Failing that, all law firms had offices in the same area of Glasgow. They were never hard to find.

The timing of the meeting would have given me time for a morning run, but my need to pay the rent beat my need to feel the burn. I had errands in town and invoices to drop off.

I checked myself in the bathroom mirror. Always a mistake. Never do that *before* the shower. Only do it *after*, if it's been a good shower. It was usually best to avoid the whole reflection thing until it was time to straighten your hair and apply the make-up. My father didn't teach me that. The red wine showed in my eyes, and the cigarettes came back with a rattling cough. I managed to have that perfect kind of hangover shower; the kind that freezes time and holds the water in the air around you. I'd been trying to switch to decaf coffee, but I broke the foil on a new jar of the real stuff and drank two large cups. The pastry probably wasn't strictly necessary to help chase away the hangover, but it didn't do any harm.

My Bridgeton flat used to have two bedrooms. Now it had one bedroom and an office piled with filing boxes, paperwork and old furniture. I dug out the telephone directory, but it didn't have a listing for the law firm. I fired up the ailing laptop and left it clicking over while I picked an outfit for the day. I wanted to make at least an effort to impress, so I found my best suit, a Primark special that looked like it had been ironed by a blind man, and fought with my hair for ten minutes. I checked in on the laptop, restarting it a couple of times until it worked, and then typed the name of the firm into the small search box and sent the request to the gods of Google.

It fired back the address on West Regent Street, naturally enough, and also a few news stories. I scanned through mentions of the company being started by two young upstarts, Fiona Hunter and Douglas Simpson, who had each walked out on huge jobs in the city's biggest law firm. They both posed for the camera on the steps to their office building. Two young and sickeningly attractive people, each with a perfect suit and tan. They looked just like the woman on the phone had sounded.

Money.

I downgraded my estimation and put the day at only a two on the shitey meter. My last decision before leaving the flat was an important one: heels or flats? If in doubt, the answer was always sunglasses.

I left in a good mood, choosing to ignore that I'd forgotten my keys.

Six

I walked across Glasgow Green, sucking in the fresh morning air and trying to blow away the cobwebs in my head. The Green was great in the morning, with only a smattering of joggers and dog walkers. The sun beat down on the Clyde, which looked like an actual river at the Green, not the pile of brown sludge it turned into once you got to the city.

At the other end of Glasgow Green I walked out onto Saltmarket.

This part of town looked run down, but beneath the dust and soot lay some of the finest buildings in town. Old properties in Glasgow had a habit of burning down in time for new developers to come in, but around Saltmarket and the Green you could still see the old city.

Halfway up the road, nestled between a bar and a Chinese takeaway, stood Crowther & Co., a walk-in law firm that was open to the public twenty-four hours a day. The frontage was painted white, with the firm's name in Gothic script beside an image of a skull wearing a judge's wig. The exterior gave off a very rough-and-ready impression, but the inside couldn't have been more different. Smooth and tidy, the waiting area was a narrow space made up of clean sofas that lined two walls and framed a reception desk. Behind the desk sat the receptionist, a large Ukrainian man named Alexei. He looked like a hairless bear, but he was as friendly as a puppy, always keen to please and to show off his new English words.

'Salutations, Sam.' His grin spread wide.

He looked me up and down, lingering in all the places he thought I didn't notice. Alexei was harmless, though. I didn't want to make him feel awkward.

'Hiya, Alexei, how you doing?'

'I'm spiffy.'

I had no idea what that meant, but I rolled with it. 'That's good to hear. The lord and master home?'

'Yes, go on in.'

I stepped past the desk and pushed through the door set into the wall at the rear. The room beyond was a larger space, with filing cabinets lining the walls and three desks arranged in a semicircle. Only one of the desks was occupied, though the others were piled high with papers. Fran Montgomery was in his late fifties, with a fuzzy face and the hands of a mechanic. He'd known my father, back in the day, and he'd always tried to throw business to us. He smiled at me now and waved at the empty seat in front of the desk.

'Hey, hen. What can I do for you? Is it invoice time already?'

I plucked two envelopes out of my bag as I sat down, and passed them both to him.

'Double trouble,' I said. 'The Boswell thing and the Johnny Shaw case.'

He laughed and typed something into the computer on his desk, loading up the files. 'Shaw, the guy with the paint tins?'

'Art installations, I think he called them.'

'Aye, that'll be that modern art that people talk about.'

22

'I don't know.' I leant into the chair, getting comfortable. 'I thought there was something timeless, almost classic, about the way the police cars looked when he was finished.'

He chuckled, a gentle rumble that spread from his gut and rolled upwards.

'Aye, all right. If you say so. How did the background check go?'

'Well, you can probably build something around his arresting officer. Lindsay—you've heard of him?' I waited for him to nod before proceeding. 'Yeah, fancies himself a gambler, likes to lose big in town, was seen drinking in the casino only a few hours before his shift, so the arrest itself would be questionable.'

'Could work, but it's too late. Johnny's decided to plead guilty. He says he's too proud of the work to let it go unclaimed, wants credit for it.' He scanned through my invoices for a second. 'You'll take a cheque, right?'

I raised my eyebrow, and he chuckled again before scrawling a quick signature across both and sliding them into his to-do pile. He passed me a sheet of paper and waited while I scanned down it, a divorce case that was getting messy. The marriage had ended in theft and accusations of domestic abuse.

'Fancy taking a look into the husband on that one for me? See if you can get anything?'

I folded the paper into my bag and started to stand up before thinking better of it. 'Fran, do you know anything about Hunter & Simpson? I think they want to hire me for something.'

'Oh, aye. The new breed. It's all the rage with the kids. They show up, flash some cash, take a couple of high-profile cases and get their names in the papers, take on a few celebrities as clients. Then at their first chance, they sign media deals and get onto TV and into publishing, ditch their practice. These guys are hunting out celebrity criminals, true crime cases, so they want the saucy stuff.'

'Not worth working with them?'

'Did you not listen to a word I said? Cash? Celebrities? Who wouldn't want in on that? Just remember me when you're rich, okay?'

I left with his chuckle rolling out the door after me.

Seven

Hunter & Simpson's office was on West Regent Street overlooking Blythswood Square. The grey stone front of the building looked down its nose at me as I walked up the steps; these things must have been designed specifically for solicitors.

Blythswood Square was a small, fenced-off garden which used to be one of Glasgow's most notorious red light districts. By day you'd pay to get screwed by lawyers, and by night you'd pay for the real thing. The council and cops had worked together to try and clean up the square; they'd cut back all the bushes and trees, and mounted large metal fences around the garden with gates that were locked at night. Now the hookers had moved further down the hill, towards the riverfront, and the solicitors were all a lot more tense.

Inside the front door of the building, I checked the directory, looking to see which floor the firm was on, only to find that they used all of it. The recession hadn't reached this far up the street. The reception area was decorated in muted shades of black and tan. Anything that didn't share that colour scheme was made of glass. A woman who was far too young and far too skinny greeted me. She took my name and waved me into a large waiting area.

She didn't whisper that she was a child slave or beg for help.

She didn't ask if I could sneak her a cheeseburger.

The waiting area was more comfortable than my flat, with two large leather sofas and a glass coffee table full of the morning's papers. I sat there, flicking through a newspaper, until the receptionist came back and said that Ms Hunter was ready to meet me. I checked the time on my phone: 11.23.

The receptionist led me through a glass door and up a small staircase to the top floor. It was decorated in a similar vein, but a lot of sleet grey had been added to the colour scheme, and the glass panels were frosted. She knocked on a large door straight ahead of us and then left me outside while she went in alone. She stepped back out and held the door wide for me to walk through, before shutting it after me and returning to whatever she did while she refused to eat. The office was large but minimal, a strange combination. There was a desk against the far wall, with a large window behind it. There were a sofa and coffee table along the wall to my right, and a large framed photo of Glasgow's dockyard on the left.

'Nice photo, isn't it?' The young woman who rose from behind the desk was from the news story. She looked even more expensive in the flesh, and my clothes instantly felt jealous. Her dark pin-stripe suit was pressed and tailored, and her shirt was probably silk, but I was no expert. Her fake tan was so expensive, you'd think it was real anywhere other than Glasgow, and her eyes were the sharpest blue I'd ever seen.

'It's great. Where'd you get it?'

'I took it myself.'

I gave her a second look. Photography was my real passion, and I'd been studying it at university when I'd had to quit to take over the family business. She offered me her hand for a shake, and I noticed she was wearing cufflinks. That struck me as odd. Her perfume had a masculine edge to it, a slight musk.

'Fiona Hunter,' she said. 'And you must be Ms Ireland.'

I nodded, and said, 'Yes, Sam.'

'Ireland Investigations.' She said the name of my company as if she was walking round it and kicking the tyres. 'That's a brave name in this town.'

'I suppose my dad was making a point when he chose it.'

She looked at me again for a second, as if she was placing me from a memory. 'I've seen you. Out on the Green on a Saturday, maybe? Are you a runner?'

I smiled. 'Yes. You won't see me on the Green on a Saturday morning, though. I go there at night to unwind. It's right by my flat.'

'Pollok Park, then? Parkrun? What's your PBT?'

'I've been sneaking in just under twenty for the last few weeks. I'm pushing for nineteen, but it keeps beating me.'

'Twenty minutes is a great time. Six-minute miles? Getting any faster than that is hard going.' She gave me a smile, and I knew what was coming. 'I'm at seventeen minutes.'

Runners. 'Well done,' I said through gritted teeth. We pretend to be supportive, but really? It's all pissing up the wall. Am I faster than you? Are you fitter than me? Do you spend more money on your running shoes? I wanted to hate her for that alone.

'I liked what you did with that insurance case.' She saved me from plotting her slow murder on the running track. 'And the way you tried to avoid the publicity. That's a quality we admire.'

I'd picked up a case a few months previously that had got me some attention. An insurance firm had hired me to check over a few formalities before they paid out on a tenement building that had collapsed on London Road. It had turned out to be more involved, and I'd set the ball rolling for the police on what turned into a major fraud investigation. The newspapers had come calling, but I'd stayed discreet and refused to talk to them. Now didn't seem like the right time to tell Ms Hunter that the only principle I'd been holding out for was the one called *the right price*.

'Discretion like that is better than any business card. Your name is coming up at all the right dinners. We're in a similar position right now.' She paused for a moment, and I wondered if she was waiting for me to say something, but then she continued. 'We've had some success in our dealings, and we're looking to expand the business, take on new people. After seeing that you know how to handle things, we would like to give you a try.'

Give you a try. She actually said that, like testing a car. My need to pay the rent was slowly giving way to the need to make cheap points.

'I don't really do test drives.'

She stopped me short. 'You're not interested?'

Was I? Hell yes.

'Naturally, I—'

She stopped me short again by turning and walking back to her desk. She sat behind it and waved for me to take the opposite seat, which I did.

'I'm going to level with you, Sam,' she said. 'My partner, Douglas—he has a lot of family connections in town. There are a lot of people he wants to bring in, established investigators, people who've been around for years and already know all the right hand-shakes. Not people I want to do business with if I can help it. They make my skin crawl. I'm pushing hard for you to be given the chance. I'm hoping you won't let me down.'

I didn't say yes, but I didn't need to. She placed a manila envelope on the desk and slid it towards me.

'What is it?'

A very expensive shrug. I wondered if they taught them at rich school. 'Legal papers. Boring, really. Have you heard of Rab Anderson?' I nodded. Anderson was a Glasgow celebrity. Which is one way of saying *dangerous*. She continued. 'There's a craze at the moment. True crime memoirs. These guys like to get paid for admitting in print things they used to dispute in court. We spend more time these days dealing with publishers than we do with prosecutors, but there's money in it, so we're not complaining. Anderson's on his third book, and one of our clients is taking legal action, but we can't find him to serve the papers.'

Did I really want approval from a rich lawyer badly enough to tangle with one of the South Side's best-selling authors?

Did I really want to be employed by someone who could do 5K so much quicker than me?

Hunter smiled at me and started talking money, and I decided, yes—yes, I did.

Eight

After leaving the office, I called my big brother. Then called him again when it went to voicemail. Then a third time, and he picked up.

'I was asleep.' He sounded like he still was.

'It's midday, Philomena. What are you doing in bed?'

'Sleeping.'

Philip was my younger brother. But he was built like an out-of-shape bouncer, so we agreed that he was my *big* brother. Technically, he was an equal partner in the business, but he wanted to have as little to do with it as possible. It interfered with his life of comic books, WWE and gay porn. His main contributions were to drive me around whenever and wherever I wanted, because I was probably the only private investigator in the world who couldn't legally drive.

'What's the job?'

'Serving papers, what else?' I paused while a couple of cars drove past, and the sound bounced around the street. 'You should have seen the woman who hired me, Phil. She probably gets somebody to come and sweep the road before she walks down it, to keep the dust off her feet.'

'For real?'

'Different class. Big time.'

'Then what's she doing talking to you?'

'Funny. And true. She says the insurance case has got us a good rep. Wants me on retainer, but I'm being tested out first. Phil, this could be the one. Get this right, and maybe we'll get an office back.'

I wondered if being on retainer at Hunter & Simpson would come with office space, a nice glass desk and a receptionist—maybe? I'd even feed mine from time to time.

'Where do you need me to pick you up?' Phil sounded close to the phone, like it was cradled in his neck or he was lying on the phone in bed.

'Not yet. I'm going to call Andy first, get a lead on where to start looking. You get out of bed, though. I'll be needing a ride soon.'

He made a noise that was neither yes nor no. He said something that sounded like *call me* and hung up. Probably going back to sleep. I dialled another number into my phone, but it rang out to voicemail. I tried again, and this time a very irritated male voice answered, 'What?'

'Hi, Andy. Where are you?'

'Working.'

Andy Lambert was my pet cop. He pretended not to like me, but we both knew he was lying. Or we both knew I was deluded. It was definitely one or the other.

'Hey, you know what? I'm working too. Actual case. And see, I was thinking—'

'That you should hit me up for a favour.'

31

'Andy, you know what? You should be a detective.'

'Funny.' He sighed. 'What do you need?'

'I'm looking for Rab Anderson.'

There was a pause. I heard him breathing a second; then he spoke again. 'Sam, Anderson's dangerous. You should stick to insurance jobs.'

'You know that and I know that, but let's not tell the rich lady who wants to throw money at me to find him, okay?'

'Fine. I'll ask around. Call me back in ten minutes.'

'You in town?'

'Aye. Down at the Squinty Bridge.'

The Squinty Bridge was one of the many bridges that crossed the Clyde. Officially its name was the Clyde Arc, and it had been opened a decade ago with much fanfare. It crossed the river at an angle, and rising above it was a large silver arch that lit up at night. No matter how impressive a feat it was, the fact that it wasn't straight would forever leave people assuming the architect had been drunk, and the 'squinty' nickname was there to stay. In my heels it would have taken over twenty minutes, but I'd brought a pair of trainers in my bag, and I managed to walk it in just shy of fifteen minutes.

Always racing myself.

I found the police at the base of the bridge's north side. Where the water, rust and concrete showed an older and nastier side of the city. White tape had already closed off the pathway. The focus of attention was a small inlet in the riverside, broken wooden steps on a metal frame that led down into the water. The lab guys walked round in their white outfits and tried to look important, but I couldn't help noticing they didn't seem to be putting in much effort.

In the centre of the non-activity stood DI Andy Lambert. He was a hot mess. Middle age was settling in and turning his

Sunday-league footballer frame into something that was preparing itself for a paunch. His strong jawline was starting to get rounder and weaker, and his shoulders were developing the slouch of someone who now knew what he would be doing every day until he died. He never stood close enough to the razor, and he always looked like he had a drink in him. In spite of all that, he still had *something*. It was that thing that makes you look at a guy three times and then, on the third time, think, *Yes, but would it be worth the trouble?*

Even though he'd been waiting for me to turn up, he played surprised and annoyed. Well, he played surprised. I think the other was genuine.

He had a bandage wrapped around the palm of his right hand and winced a little as I handed him a warm Starbucks. I made my nicest innocent smile. 'Hiya. Whatcha got here?'

He stood to one side and pointed down the steps. Tangled up in weeds where the water lapped at the metal was a pallid, meaty lump that had once been a man. The guys in the white overalls were carrying what looked like a large plastic bag down to where the body lay.

'Floater?'

'Not sure yet. We'll know when we get him out, but the techies are creaming themselves in hope it's a murder. I'll let them play for a wee bit, then tell them he's going down on the file as a jumper.'

'How many of these do you get?'

'Difficult to say. Most people who go in around here will come out at sea, or broken up further down. By then it's hard to figure out what happened. Usually, if they've gone in upriver, they get caught in the tidal weir.'

'You make those calls for me?'

He turned to face me fully. He was making a show, pretending that he maybe wasn't going to help me. 'And what makes you think I'll just roll over every time and give you what you need?'

'Well,' I pushed back. 'There is that thing—'

He pointed his finger in my face, Harrison Ford style. 'Three times.' His jaw tensed, and he lowered his voice. 'It was just three times.'

'More like two and a half, really. But actually I was going to say you should help me because you liked my dad, and you wouldn't want his business going under, would you?'

He shook his head and then laughed at something in the distance. My father had been on the force before going private. He'd always said that in order to get anywhere as a cop in Glasgow, you needed to know the right handshakes and the right songs. It was a city of football, religion and Masons, in that order. My father had been on the wrong side of each of those divides, but he'd made friends along the way. Lambert was one of them.

'Yeah. I called Vic in vice. He says Anderson's a tough one to pin down these days unless there's a book launch.' He handed me a piece of paper that I slipped into my jacket pocket. 'But that's his last known address, and Vic says you might catch him in one of the pubs at Cessnock: the Park Bar or the Pit. You know where they are?'

I did.

I pointed to the dressing on his hand. 'Cut yourself shaving? You know you're meant to hold the razor the other way around, right?'

He looked down at it, then put the hand in his pocket.

'Accident at home,' he said.

I turned to leave, but he touched my arm. 'You're going to take Phil along with you, aye?'

'Philomena? What's he going to do if things get rough—sing them show tunes as a distraction while I run away?'

'So he's camp as Christmas, but he looks like a tough bastard, and that's what counts with these people. They see you coming on your own and—well, they'll see you coming.'

I smiled at him as I walked away, asked him to say hi to his wife for me.

Nine

The Pit was a run-down single-storey building in Cessnock. Two streets back from the main road, you only made it here when you'd run out of other places to go. It was in need of either several layers of paint or a wrecking ball. Its real name was the Cessnock Bar, but over time that had become nothing but a technicality. Having *Cess* at the start of the name was too easy a target for Glaswegians to miss. At some point it had become the Cesspit and then, eventually, simply the Pit.

It said a lot about the people who drank in there that they wore the name like a badge of honour.

It was a Rangers pub and, this close to the 12 July Orange March, it had Union flags hanging in the windows. Even so many years after the smoking ban, I was still hit with the smell of tobacco as I walked in. It was a full daytime crowd, dole monkeys and old men. Each had the glassy eyes that told me he was already past his first drink of the day, and most were holding electronic cigarettes like life jackets. I was hit with a craving but swallowed it down. I tried to keep my smoking to first thing in the morning and when I was out drinking. It messed with my running if I smoked any more than that.

All the men turned to stare at me. It wasn't a comfortable feeling. I was very aware of how many of them there were and of how long it would take me to get to the door.

'All right, hen?'

The man nearest to me smiled and shuffled a little on his stool. He had the thin frame of someone who was used to choosing spirits over food. For a second it seemed like he was testing out whether or not he could stand up and sweet-talk me. The shuffle ended in defeat, and he stayed sat down. I nodded at him and got straight to the point.

'You seen Rab Anderson?'

The room fell silent. Then someone at the back of the room laughed, a gravelly sound slicked over by tobacco and mucus. I looked in the direction of the laugh, but it was too dim at the rear. I took a few steps forward, becoming very aware that each one was taking me further from the door.

' 'Sall right—we won't bite.' The gravel laugh sliced into words. 'Who is it looking for Rab?'

I steeled myself and walked over to the back of the room. The speaker was an old man, shorter than me and rail thin. He didn't look as drunk as his friends, and his clothes were crisp and clean. This was a different class of drinker. I handed him my business card, and he nodded after scanning it; said he'd heard of my dad.

'Wish we could help, but Rab's not around. He's on holiday.'

'Holiday?'

'Aye, little bit of R 'n' R down in London.'

I hated London. 'Not my idea of a holiday.'

His eyes narrowed a little. Just enough for me to notice it. They flitted away to someone behind me and then back. I felt someone step in close, but whoever it was didn't do anything other than make his presence felt.

'And why would you be after Rab, anyway?'

I shrugged. 'Oh, you know, the usual. I'd like him to sign a copy of the book.'

He pretended to believe me. 'A bit of a fan, eh? What's your favourite wan?'

'The one where he does that thing—you know, with the . . . uh, you know the one?' Thinking on my feet had always been my strong suit. 'That one where he's pretending to be a cripple, and then at the end we see he was really Keyser Söze?'

He sighed and leant back in his chair. He stared down at his beer and turned the glass around on the table a couple of times before he spoke again. 'You're funnier than the last person who came looking for him, I'll give you that, hen. But it always goes the same way.'

He nodded at whoever was behind me. Vice-like hands pulled my arms to my back and bent me forward, over the edge of the bar so that my cheek pressed into the wood. I heard a lot of dirty laughter and felt myself flush with fear and anger. The old man ripped my bag away in one sharp movement and began rifling through it. He tipped items out onto the bar top: my phone, my purse, my notebook, make-up. The chocolate bar that I liked to pretend wasn't in there. He held up the manila envelope that Fiona Hunter had given me.

'Would this be your little present for Rab?'

I mumbled something that was close enough to a yes, but I wasn't released. The old man sat back down in his chair and turned the envelope over a few times, inspecting the seal and making a show of deciding whether to open it.

'We'll play a game,' he said. 'You like games? Here's how it works. You tell me what's inside this envelope, and then I open it. If you're right, then I'll maybe tell you where to find him and you can deliver whatever it is.'

'If I'm wrong?'

'Then after you get out of hospital, you can limp back to whoever paid you to deliver this and ask them to do their own dirty work.'

That didn't seem like the kind of game I wanted to play. I tended not to join in if I knew I had no chance of winning.

'I have no idea what's in it.' I tried the honest approach. 'I'm just delivering it. It'll be a court summons—he's probably named the wrong person in a book or something.'

The old man looked disappointed and placed the envelope on the table next to his beer. 'Hen, you didn't even give me a chance to start the game. The last person who tried your job at least let us play the game before we fucked him up. Still, you were honest. He wasn't. I'll give you that.'

He nodded at whoever was holding me down, and I felt the weight shift behind me as if I were about to take a nasty kick. I pulled myself to the side and managed to twist free while my attacker was off balance. I righted myself and turned round. The man who had been holding me was actually a woman. Short and stocky, with big shoulders. She was like the schoolyard dinner lady from hell. As she turned back to swing at me, I grabbed my mobile phone off the counter and pressed it into her neck. I gambled that I'd been quick enough that all anyone knew was that I'd grabbed something sleek and black.

'Taser,' I said. 'Move and I zap. I'm told it's pretty dangerous to get someone in the neck, but I'm not a doctor, so who knows, maybe it doesn't hurt.'

She froze. So did everybody else. The old man sucked on his electronic cigarette and let the water vapour out into the air above him. He watched me and waited for my next move.

39

I was also waiting for it. I was frankly hoping an idea would be along any second.

That's when my phone started to ring.

Ten
Lambert

The corpse was pasty and sodden. If someone had a heart attack or a stab wound, Lambert knew, you couldn't tell straight away whether they were dead. You needed to get down close to them, check the vitals, look for life before assuming death. When you pulled someone out of the water, you knew straight away if they were gone. They were pale and sodden, heavy with water, and they looked more like a fleshy object than a human being. Something essential was missing.

The only catch was that the water could keep decomposition from setting in fully. It could be difficult to tell how long a stiff had been in there. On the plus side, there was also none of the farting you tended to get with dry bodies. Lambert knew from experience that dead people were rude like that.

He knelt down and looked at the stiff as it was laid out on the plastic sheet. The labbies wouldn't take it further away until they'd had a chance to examine the scene, searched for any other pieces of information in the right context, as if it wasn't already obvious how this guy had died.

Lambert could never figure out why someone would want to go that way. Not with a choice of options. Gunshot? Fine. Jump off a building? Okay. At least it would be over in a few seconds, and you would get to experience flying, albeit very badly.

But drowning?

Sinking into cold water, not knowing how long it would be before you died? The human body was a persistent fucker. It fought to stay alive. You could be in the water for a long time before you finally faded to black, and it was going to hurt—you were going to have to fight against your own instincts all the way to death. Worse, maybe you'd live, but your brain would've been starved of oxygen for too long and you'd be a vegetable, never able to take a second attempt at ending it all. Living out your days in a hospital bed, someone cleaning out your piss and shit, with you just conscious enough to experience every waking moment of it.

No thanks.

Not for Lambert.

Living into middle age was starting to be torture enough, trying to hold onto a job and keep his father-in-law off his back, without losing the ability to drink or screw.

He looked down into the face of the dead body and shook his head.

'You stupid fucker,' he said.

'What was that, boss?'

Callum, the head labbie, turned round at the sound of Lambert's voice, assuming he was being spoken to. In his white plastic overalls, with a hood tight to his head, he looked like the ghost of E.T. He was smart in all the wrong ways, in ways that Lambert couldn't understand. Callum could tell you where you'd been, based on the dirt on your shoes, but he couldn't tell a joke or understand football.

'I was talking to him.' Lambert waved at the corpse. 'He was just telling me a good joke.'

'Boss, you know he's dead, right?'

'Really?'

'Oh, wait.' Callum paused, sensing his mistake, but with no show of emotion. 'You were joking. Okay.'

Then the farting started. A long, low and smelly release of gas from the corpse. It was unusual for this type of stiff to release gas in that way, but dead bodies did unusual things all the time. It sounded wet and nasty, and everyone beat a retreat to the roadside.

'You're going to try and use this,' Lambert said to Callum. 'You're going to be tempted to say the farting is proof that it wasn't a suicide somehow. I can see it in your eyes. A guy eats too many baked beans before he goes into the sludge, farts a little when we pull him out, and you're going to add to my workload by saying it's a suspicious death.'

Callum stared at Lambert for a long time before replying in monotone, 'Another joke? You're on form today.'

'No, I'm serious this time. Do what you want. Play—have some fun with him—but when the paperwork hits my desk, it says suicide, okay?'

Lambert walked away before Callum could respond. He'd learnt a long time ago that the key to management was to issue a command and then get moving before anyone could disagree with it. He headed back up to the road, where his car was parked. A few uniforms were directing traffic and turning away the pedestrians. One of them leant over to open Lambert's car door, like a real suck-up. Lambert nodded and smiled, pretended to have noticed the guy's face. They were sucking up to the wrong person. Lambert was not in a position to do them any favours. But, hell, if someone wanted to think you'd remember them, fine; you might get something out of it.

Lambert sat down in the driver's seat and felt the mistake straight away; he'd been awake for over twenty-four hours, and it all started to catch up with him as he sank back into the cushion. He opened his eyes and took in a deep breath, getting the air pumping around his body. It wasn't bedtime yet; he had a couple more errands to run.

He needed coffee.

He needed bacon.

He needed a bottle of Talisker.

Lambert had skipped the chance to clock off an hour ago. He'd been at the end of his shift when the call came in about a floater in the river. He could have passed it off to Cummings or Harper and gone home. But there were certain unwritten rules on the job that never changed. He'd been the one to take the call, so it was on his plate. Break a written rule and people noticed—they judged you; but break an unwritten rule, and they never forgave you.

Lambert picked up the radio receiver and called dispatch, advised them the floater was out of the river and the case was under his name, that any enquiries should be forwarded to his mailbox. Then he checked his phone and saw two messages from Jess.

Fucking kids. Ryan Lindsay just bit Sherry Mitchell. Drew blood. Maybe you could come and arrest them, throw away the key? XX

Can't reach Ryan's parents on the phone. He keeps talking about this bike he wants for his birthday. I might be serious about you arresting him, BTW. Want anything from the shop on the way home? XX

Jess was a primary schoolteacher, spending her day dealing with screaming children before going home to a usually empty house.

44

It was never easy being married to a cop, and Jess caught it worse than many others. They'd been together for seventeen years, married for fifteen of those, and children had never been a factor. Jess always said she spent her days surrounded by kids and didn't want to fill her nights with them too. That had worked fine for Lambert. He liked the freedom. He'd always seen two kinds of men: those who never had kids and could stay eighteen forever, and those who became parents and turned forty-five overnight.

No thanks.

Lately he was seeing a third kind. His kind. The men who never figured themselves out. Sliding into middle age with no plan and no direction, finding alcohol and double shifts at work the best way to fill the silence in their own heads.

Thinking of life with Jess played another trick on him. It made him think of Sam, and for a moment he felt younger again. He keyed the ignition with his right hand as he dialled Sam's number with his left.

Time to go play the good guy.

Eleven

Sam answered after a few rings.

'DI Lambert, how can I help?'

She must have seen his number on the screen. There was tension in her voice. It didn't suit her. Something was going on. Surely she hadn't just walked round to the Pit and gone in on her own without calling her brother for backup?

'Where are you?' Lambert asked.

'Hang on.' The line got muffled for a second, and Sam could be heard talking to someone else, saying, 'This is important. I need to take it.' Then back to Lambert: 'I'm in the Pit. I believe you know the place?'

Idiot. She'd really done it. She was just like her father, except smaller and female, and less able to fight. But as far as the stubborn and reckless streaks went, they could have been the same person. Lambert didn't know whether to be angry or proud. He settled for both.

'Everything okay?'

'Hmmmmmmm?'

That told him all he needed to know. 'On my way.'

Lambert ran traffic lights on both sides of the Squinty Bridge, and then again on Govan Road as he drove around the edge of Festival Park. Every cop secretly wanted to squeal tyres and perform handbrake turns, and as he approached the Pit, he was planning to do just that, but he saw Sam was already out the door and running in the opposite direction.

She was a good runner, strong and fast, with a sprint that was damn near Olympic. Lambert overtook her and pulled in at the kerb, leaning over to open the passenger door. She dropped into the seat, hardly out of breath.

'Don't say it,' she said.

'That I told you so?'

'Yes, don't say it.'

Lambert smiled, waited a second before playing it cool. 'You okay?'

'I was doing okay until you called. I'd got them thinking my phone was a Taser, was about to gather up all my stuff and walk out of there all classy-like, but then you went and ruined it.'

'You're welcome.'

She looked at Lambert, out of the corner of her eye at first, then head on, a smile spreading across her face. 'I'm joking. Thanks. You saved my arse.' Then she raised a finger in the space between them. 'Avoid the obvious joke, for once.'

'Sure. As long as you're okay.'

'Embarrassed, mostly. They've got all my stuff. My bag, my purse, my address. At least I left my keys at home. And, shit, they've got the legal papers I'm meant to serve on Anderson. I'm going to be fired from a job I only took an hour ago.'

'Look,' Lambert said, 'shit happens. Don't worry about it. I'll go get your stuff—they know not to mess with me. Can't promise your purse will have anything in it, though. Wait here.' He opened the door and started to climb out before hesitating. 'Sam, I mean it; don't do anything daft, okay?'

She gave him an innocent angel look, putting both hands out. 'Me?'

Lambert walked towards the Pit. There were smokers outside, hardened old men who'd lived through the rougher days of the city, men who'd maybe been willing to mess with cops when they were younger. None of them wanted to be the first to budge, but there was enough room between them for Lambert to pass through.

Inside, his eyes adjusted quickly to the dim light. Murdo was at the back, sitting in his usual spot. He was thin these days. There was a time when he'd been built like an athlete, with strong arms and shoulders for beating the crap out of people who crossed him, but now he was a broken-down survivor who knew not to mess with the wrong people.

'She with you?' Murdo said. 'Comes round here asking about Rab, thinks she can just walk in and out without a beating?'

'She can.' Lambert's voice was calm, unworried. 'She's under my protection. And you'll give me her belongings. All of them.'

'Will I now?'

Murdo's tobacco-aged lips turned up in a grin. The room closed in around Lambert as the smokers stepped in behind him. On anyone else it would be intimidation, but Lambert was a cop and knew it for what it was: angry children trying to pretend they could stare down the adult in the room before looking away.

He gave them their moment before putting them back in their box.

'You done?'

Murdo nodded to the bar, and a squat old lady placed Sam's bag on the counter, and beside it the manila envelope of legal papers. It had been opened.

'I think we need to talk about Rab,' Murdo said.

'Not here,' Lambert said. He nodded at the bag. 'It better all be there.'

He gathered up what he'd come for and headed back out of the bar, calm and slow. When he got to the car, Sam was in the driver's seat. She waited for Lambert to sit in the passenger's seat and turned the ignition.

'Where can I drop you?' She said it with a sly smile.

'Fancy a quick drink?'

'Maybe.'

'That's a "no", isn't it?'

She pulled away from the kerb. 'Uh-huh.'

Lambert waited a few hundred yards to see which direction she was heading in. She turned along the Clyde River and back towards the city, past the BBC building.

'This is dangerous,' Lambert said. 'Can I convince you to drop it?'

'That's also a "maybe".'

'Well, at least be careful, okay? Don't go anywhere without backup. Rab goes to ground whenever there's trouble, and his friends will hand a beating out to anyone who comes looking. It's how people like Rab survive so long.'

They drove through The Gorbals. Lambert had seen these streets change a lot over his years on the job. Old brown tenements and Gothic churches had fallen victim to the Glasgow 'disease' and burned down to make way for new developments. Apartment blocks and houses were springing up along the old roads, with bright colours and balconies as if a view of the Clyde added value to anything. They crossed the river at the end of Ballater Street, onto the road that cut through Glasgow Green, and Lambert knew where they were headed but stayed silent.

They passed through the roughest part of Bridgeton, an old Ulster loyalist neighbourhood, and onto a quiet modern housing estate that was hidden away in the wreckage like a well-kept secret.

Sam parked in front of her flat.

'Want that quick drink?' she asked.

Twelve

Forty minutes later Lambert pulled the front door closed behind him and stepped back over to his car. If he'd been tired before, he was exhausted now. He had a few extra aches and that pleasant numb feeling you get right after emptying your dick. He should have taken a shower, but he was in a hurry to run his last errand.

One final thing he needed to do; then his own bed would be calling him.

He unlocked the car and clicked on the radio, contacting dispatch to sign off for the day. He'd had a voicemail from Callum saying he wasn't ready to call the floater a suicide just yet. Great. Another problem to fix.

He drove back into The Gorbals, down Ballater Street to the old train arches. He turned off the road behind a boarded-up pub that had stood empty since the credit crunch, and walked over to a forgotten garage lock-up that was built into the archway of the overpass. He fiddled with the rusted padlock for a moment, having to fight with it before he could unlock it, then slipped inside and pulled the door closed.

There was a bolt on the inside of the door, and he slid it home to make sure there wouldn't be any unexpected visitors.

He felt around on the floor for the lamp he'd left there last night, and fired it up. The batteries were low, and the halogen blinked a little, but the beam filled up the room round him.

He smiled at Rab Anderson.

Anderson was tied down on a wooden door that was acting as a bed. He was a faded tattoo of his younger self. A strong man gone soft with age. Even old men can put up a fight when they're being tortured, though, and he carried the wounds. His kneecaps were broken, and one of his hands was crushed and folded inwards like a dead spider. His mouth was covered with gaffer tape, but with all the morphine in his system he was doing nothing other than breathing and occasionally grunting.

His grunting started to form into something regular and solid. Lambert knelt down and pulled back the gaffer tape. Anderson didn't miss a beat as the tape ripped away, but kept on mumbling. He was praying, in slurred, half-remembered words. There was a sing-song element to the way he talked. It must have been difficult not to sound like an idiot, with missing teeth and a system full of drugs.

Lambert screwed the tape up into a ball and pocketed it. The extra movement snapped Anderson back into the room, and he stared at Lambert with clear eyes.

'Motherfucker,' Anderson said.

'Good to see you too, Rab.' Lambert said. 'No need to get up; I won't be here long.'

'Try untying me. See how long you last.'

Lambert nodded. 'Sorry, Rab.' He pulled rubber gloves from his pocket and slipped them on, forcing one over the bandage on his hand. 'You wouldn't believe how hard I tried to avoid this. Really. But people are starting to ask questions, and I can't have you waiting around to be found and identify us. It's nothing personal.'

He picked up the roll of gaffer tape from the floor and ripped off a fresh strip. Rab's eyes widened as Lambert leant in, but he had nowhere to pull back to. He mumbled something else and Lambert held off for a moment.

'What was that?'

Rab's mouth opened and closed, and another drugged-up prayer started, but then he found the words he was looking for and, like a lost child, whispered, 'I want my dog.'

Lambert pressed the tape down over Anderson's mouth and smoothed it out. The lips beneath the tape were taking up the rhythmic mumbling again. Lambert pinched Anderson's nose with his right hand while pressing down on the tape, making sure it was sealed. Anderson's eyes spread wide and he tried to fight back, even through the drugs, shaking his head from side to side.

Eventually the light started to go out behind his eyes.

'The things we do for family,' Lambert said right before Anderson died. 'You know how it is.'

PART TWO

'Never trust a psychiatrist to treat a bullet wound.'

—*Mackie*

Thirteen
Mackie

Lately I've been watching a lot of TV shows about crimes. *Columbo. Rockford. Quincy.* Shit like that. I've got a handle on how to do this. Someone grabbed my Uncle Rab and killed his dog. They put a bullet in my leg and killed Jenny T. I'm going to solve this.

Detective Mackie.

Every great detective has to start somewhere: I decide on the last place I saw Rab. We were both drinking in the Pit before he suggested I go get my dick wet to work off some frustration. If he stayed there after I left, then maybe the guys who were with us will have an idea what happened to him.

I tell Beth to pull to the kerb as we drive through Cessnock. She looks over at me with that bit of hair falling across her face again. She looks scared.

'Where are you going?'

'Got a few things to take care of. Won't be long.'

'But what about'—she nods towards the bundle on the back seat—'you know.'

'Oh yeah, the wee man. Take him back to yours, aye? I'll come round later on, and we'll find a nice spot to bury him, say some words.' Then I think of something. Fuck-a-doodle-do, I can be an idiot sometimes. 'Hey, did you pick up the keys at Rab's flat?'

'What keys?'

'His fucking house keys, what else?'

She looks at me blank, like I've just asked her the capital of Constantipopple. Baws. That means the keys are wherever I left them. And I have no idea where that is. Nothing I can do about it now. I'll square it all later. Beth starts to talk again, and she's still at it as I shut the door and limp away. She's a talker. That's the problem with psychiatrists. They want to talk about every fucking thing.

I'm trying not to let my wound show in my walk—don't want people to see any weakness—but it's hard. With every other step, I lose feeling in my leg for a bit, like my body keeps forgetting it's there. I'm no expert, but I don't think that's normal. I duck into the newsagent by the subway to get a pack of cigs and a bottle of Buckie. Didn't want to spark up or drink in front of Beth; she'd get all upset if I do that after taking my pills.

Which reminds me.

I head over to the street at the back, out of sight from the main road, and heave until one of the pills coughs up out of my throat and onto the pavement. Damn, the other one must've actually gone in. Ach well, maybe one won't hurt.

I walk round to the Pit. The classiest shithole in the city. Or the nearest anyway. As I push through the door, everyone turns to stare at me, like in a movie. Their drinks are frozen in place at their lips. They don't half look stupid.

''Sup, dudes.' I wave. 'Someone get me a pint.'

Murdo is at the back, trying to look like he's still tough and not an old jakey. He's sat beside some dykey-looking woman. She looks familiar, like maybe I was introduced to her last night, but my memory don't work right after a few pints. There's quite a lot of last night that I don't remember. Either way, it looks like she knows me, because she nods as I walk over. Murdo is mooching through a woman's purse, which is strange, but then he's a strange guy.

'Mackie, son, you look like you've been shot.'

'Aye.'

I leave it there, like that, see how he responds. He smiles and hits the table with the palms of his hands before laughing.

'Should have known,' he says between laughs. 'You were looking like you wanted to start trouble when you left here. You put a few away last night, son.'

I think of the guys I killed, and Jenny T as she splattered all over me. 'A few what?'

He puts his head to one side and smiles. 'Drinks. You all right, son?'

'No, I'm not. I got shot. And now I can't find Uncle Rab.'

His lips pucker and open like a fish a couple times. Then he plays with an envelope on the table, turning it round. 'Not you as well.' He points to the purse. 'Was that your girlfriend we just got rid of?'

'What?'

'Lass came in here, looks like one of them drama students that go on the sub crawl and get lost. She was asking for him too. Haven't seen him since last night. He left not long after you.'

'Aye? Well, I saw him here with you last night, and now I can't find him. His place has been turned over too. Any idea where he was going? Any idea where he is right now?'

His eyes narrow, and he tries to find a little of the old *Murdo Murder* spirit. 'Whatcha sayin', son?'

'I think you know.'

He shakes his head and waves, dismissing me. 'Away with you. Go sleep this mood off before you say the wrong thing.'

I feel people around me stand up, ready to force it if I don't behave. I see the woman crack her knuckles together and smile a

61

little. I can take each and every one of them if I have to. Then I feel my leg, blinking on and off like a faulty Christmas light, and I put my hands out. 'Aye, all right. Okay.'

I turn and walk out. It takes everything I've got not to let the limp show as I move. I save that up till I'm outside and buckle against the wall, rubbing my thigh like Beth did, but I don't have her magic blond hair or English accent, so it doesn't make me feel any better. Once I'm feeling up to it, I head round the back. The Pit used to be the ground floor of a tenement building, but the rest of it was demolished after a fire. The Pit itself now stands on its own, the space behind it that had been the backyard now just a mess of broken concrete and weeds.

I find the window to the lav. I know it from all the times I've dropped something out of it during a police raid. I slip the kitchen knife from Rab's place out of my pocket and slide it into the gap where the window opens outward, working it loose until I can get a grip with my fingers. Then it's easy enough to slip in through the window.

I sit and wait there. I don't know how long. I get the urge to pee a couple times but hold it in. Third time I figure, what the hell? I'm in the right place for it. Just as I'm finishing up, I hear movement the other side of the door, and I slip back out of sight just as it opens.

Murdo walks past, not sensing me there, and pulls his tackle out, pointing it at the steel urinal. Before he can relax enough to let rip, I step in beside him and grab his wee boaby, gripping it hard and twisting a little. He yelps and pulls away, but then realises that's going to cause him more pain, so he steps closer. It must be tricky trying to figure out what to do when a man has grabbed your dick in a lav. Almost as weird as being the guy holding it. I've only ever touched my own until now. His piece is warmer than I'd expected. Rougher too. It's like holding one of those battered sausages in a chip shop.

I make his decision easy and show him the kitchen knife in my other hand, bringing it close to his wee man. He gets the message.

'You must have me confused,' I tell him, 'with the man who fucks about.'

He doesn't speak, so I prompt him and he nods. 'Yeah, sorry, won't happen again.'

'It's okay, no problem,' I tell him, being nice, reasonable. 'All I want to know is where Rab is.'

'I don't know, mate. I really don't.'

'See, the thing is now I have to cut your dick off, aye? I mean, I'm trying here, Murdo, I really am. I want to leave you be. But then, my uncle has gone missing, someone's killed his dog, and two fuckers shot at me last night, so my patience is wearing a bit thin. And hey'—I look down into my hands—'speaking of thin.'

'Okay, okay, look.' His breathing is coming really brittle, and I don't know whether I'm more worried that he'll piss on me or have a heart attack. 'After you went last night, he got a call on his mobile, said it was from Gary Fraser. Then he left.'

'Fraser? What the fuck would Rab want with him?'

'He didn't say.'

A fella has a way of telling the truth when you're tugging on his boaby, so I let go. He relaxes and forgets what's about to happen. The piss splashes all over his trousers and shoes.

I laugh, wash my hands and walk out through the door. All his people get to their feet, but they're torn. Do they rush me or run to the toilet to see what I've done to their boss? They don't choose either, just hovering there, caught between the two. 'I think your man needs a towel,' I say as I strut my way out of the bar.

Fourteen

R ight.

Gary Fraser.

I know him. Bought some righteous weed from him. Some shit too, but overall he comes out on top. But Uncle Rab isn't a fan of the puff. Why would he be talking with Gaz?

One way to find out.

I usually find Gaz sat at the bar in Lebowskis, working his way through cocktails while pretending to be all manly about it. I swear I even saw him have a drink with an umbrella in it once. It's a twenty-minute walk, I reckon, but with my fucked-up leg, maybe longer. It takes me around the edge of Festival Park and then across the Squinty Bridge. At the other side of the bridge, I see a load of police tape and them wankers in white outfits gathered around the back of a van. I look the other way, try not to be noticed.

If you don't feel nervous when you see a copper, there's something wrong with you.

My leg goes to sleep while I'm looking the other way, and I fall over.

Nice and subtle, aye? A uniformed copper helps me to my feet, asks if I'm okay. I decide now is not the time to tell him to fuck off and suck dick in hell, so I just say, 'Aye, thanks,' and walk on up the hill. At the top of Finnieston Street, I cross the road and turn away from the city. Lebowskis is just a little further down, perched on the corner of the block like a beacon for alcoholics. It's one of they places where, when you walk in, you know they're serious about selling you booze. There's tons of the stuff, and it's all arranged nice on shelves behind the bar. I don't think it's weird to say that walking into a place like this gets my dick hard.

Gary Fraser is sat at the bar. He raises a drink to me and nods. He's not one for words. Unless he's on the Jägerbombs; then he won't shut up. He's a bit shorter than me, and more laid back. Likes to look cool and down with the kids in jeans and designer tops. He used to have spiky hair, loads of that gel, but now he's trying to look all grown up and it's combed flat to his head, parted on the side like one of they models on telly.

'All right,' he says.

'No,' I say. 'Some cunt shot me in the leg.'

He looks impressed. Leans back from the bar to take a good look at me. 'Which one?'

I tap the wound. It doesn't hurt, and I'm sure that's not a good sign. My trackie feels a bit wet, and I hope I'm not bleeding again.

Gary smiles. 'Not going to be doing any tap dancing for a while then?'

I ask the barman for a shot of tequila. I slam it down and ask for another. My brain gets a nice buzz on the go. I ask for a third and slam that one away too, before turning back to Gary.

'I'd offer you a drink,' he says. 'But it looks like you know where the bar is.'

'You saw Rab last night.'

'I did.' He nodded. 'Came here just before closing.'

'Why would Rab come to you? He doesn't like drugs.'

'I'm a man of many talents. Diverse portfolio. I do DVDs, clothes. I do guns too.'

Guns, eh? Funny that. Glasgow's not famous for guns, but Rab goes to talk to Gaz, then I get shot. Is that a coincidence? I realise I'm thinking when I could be asking.

'Rab comes to talk to you about guns,' I say. 'And I get shot. Funny.'

'I wouldn't have thought you'd laugh very much at that.' He tries for a joke. 'No, he didn't come to me for a gun. I only said that because of you, thought maybe you'd want one, with being shot and everything.'

'Why the fuck would I want a gun? Would you ask a man who's just been bitten by a shark if he wants to buy a shark?'

'Fair point. Okay. Rab was here asking for money.'

'You do loans?'

'No, but it's because of that diverse portfolio I was telling you about. He said a guy who sells drugs and guns is going to be able to get his hands on money quicker than a bookie or a bank.'

'Was he right?'

He smiles. 'Maybe.' Then he sips his drink.

'How much was he asking for?'

Gaz gets his serious face on now, puts his pint down on the bar and slides it away before shaking his head and looking at me. 'That's confidential.'

'Do I look like someone who gives a toss about the Data Protection Act?'

I do not.

'You do not.'

'Well, then,' I say, 'stop arsing about and just tell me what's going on.'

Gaz puts his hand up to say okay, okay. 'Look, I don't know. He asked if I could get sixty grand in cash. He said all his money's tied up in property and he's not going to be getting another publishing royalty for three months—he can't get his hands on the cash.'

'So he came to the bank of Gaz.'

'For a return of double next week, aye.'

'You give it to him?'

'Not yet. I agreed to get it for today. I've been waiting here for him to call.'

So the money's here? Damn. I should have played it cool, called his bluff and said Rab had sent me. Trouble is, I'm new at all this. I have no idea about investigating shit. Then again, what do I want with sixty grand? I just want to find the cunt who shot Rab's dog.

What next? Play dumb.

'And Rab hasn't called yet?'

'Nope. And from the look of your leg, I get the feeling he's not going to.'

True. But somebody might. And they might want the cash. I grab a pen from behind the bar and write Beth's mobile number on a napkin.

'If anyone calls about the money, arrange to meet them here, and leave me a message, aye?'

Gaz shrugs, pulls out his phone and waves it at me.

'Sure, might be a laugh,' he says.

Fifteen

Why would Rab need sixty grand in such a hurry? And why did I know nothing of this if I was with him last night? Who else would know about the money? My new career as a detective is just leading to more questions.

There's his accountant, Robin. He works out of an office on Blythswood Square. He's the real deal. Suit and tie. Knows all about the taxes and stuff. But he's for the money that Rab admits to. If Rab wanted money that quick, it wouldn't be for anything legit.

I need to talk to his *real* accountant.

Gilbert Neil works out of the Horse Shoe Bar in town. Him and Rab have worked together for years. If dodgy deals are going down, Gilbert knows about them. I take a cab because my leg is really starting to fuck me about now, and my hips and back keep going numb too.

Gilbert's from South Africa, though you can't tell from his accent. He moved over when he was a teenager and now sounds pure Scottish. I bet my accent wouldn't change if I went to South Africa. But why would I want to go there? It's all sun and guns. And big sharks. Fuck that. Gilbert used to be a mad keen cyclist until he had a run-in with the Calton Tong a few years ago, and now he's a mad keen sitter. He's been keeping an eye on Rab's real finances for as long as I can remember, advising on what to declare to the taxman and what to keep under the bed.

The Horse Shoe is hidden away in Drury Street, a cobbled lane just off Renfield Street, near the main train station. I keep being told that it's world famous, but I only ever see the same bunch of people in there. It's not exactly full of tourists. They serve three-course meals for the cost of a pint, and they never kick you out if you've had too much to drink. If you like seeing drunks falling off their stools, and middle-aged women belting out karaoke, this is the place for you.

Gilbert likes both of those things.

There's the ground-floor bar, but Gilbert is never in that one. I climb the brown wooden stairs that lead to the upstairs bar, and let my eyes get used to the dim light. The owner of the pub has commissioned portraits of the most regular customers and hung them on the wall near to where each of them usually sits. I can see Gilbert's shiny bald head from across the room, sat beneath his own portrait, at the corner table by the fire escape. He's around the same age as Rab, but he's kept more shape. I wouldn't want to fight him. Though we both have a dodgy leg these days, so maybe it'd be interesting. He always used to have his dog with him. A cute wee pit bull named Gojira. But the poor guy had to be put down a couple months back when his legs gave out, and Gilbert is still too gutted to replace him.

That reminds me again of Rab's dog. Every time I think of the wee man, my blood boils away a bit. I need to watch that—I might do something stupid.

He looks surprised to see me, his eyes widening for a second as they latch onto me. He's talking into a mobile phone, but he hangs up as I drop down into the seat opposite like a sack of spuds. The frame squeaks.

'You look like you've seen a ghost,' I say. 'Not expecting to see me?'

'Not in here.' He plays it cool. If he does know what's happened to me, he doesn't let on. 'You don't usually drink in here. I thought the Vale was more your kind of scene.'

'I like all kinds; I'm easy.' I pull his pint over and sip at it. It's too heavy, like a stout or something. 'So, why does Rab need sixty grand?'

Boom. Catch him right off the bat like that.

'What are you talking about, Mack?'

'Aye, you know. I just talked to Gary Fraser. He says Rab needs sixty in a hurry, nothing he can free up legally that fast, and he's going to pick it up today. You really going to pretend you don't know what it's for?'

'I honestly don't. I know he needs it, but he wouldn't say what it was for. Said it was something he was playing close to his chest, some important deal that nobody could know about until after it was done. All I know is that he needs the cash, and I'm the same as him at the moment. My money's all tied up in property deals, can't help him out.'

'You suggested Gaz?'

'Aye. Gary's helped me out a few times. As long as you get him a quick profit, he can get his hands on cash.'

Do I believe him? I don't know. He knows something more, but there's no way to beat it out of him here without attracting attention. Besides, I don't think I could. I'm already worried that I might not be able to stand up when I'm done.

'When was the last time you spoke to Rab?'

He thinks it over. That bit I believe. 'Last night—we talked on the phone. I think he was out drinking with you. He said you were talking a lot of pish, talking about your past and crying again. He mentioned he needed the cash and that's when I said he should go see Gary.'

'He say anything else?'

He doesn't answer. Instead, he looks off into the distance, pretending something over there is more distracting than me. I lean in, getting in his face but staying silent, making it uncomfortable.

'He say anything else?' I say again.

'He said he had some business to deal with at the whorehouse on Copland Road.'

Oh aye? Business to attend to in the same place I got shot?

Fuck-a-doodle-do.

Maybe it wasn't me they were after. Maybe they got me mixed up with my uncle.

I stick a cigarette in my mouth and then climb to my feet, trying not to look like a cripple. The trackie clings to my leg, and I feel the fabric sticking, needing to be pulled away as I move. Not a good sign. Never trust a psychiatrist to treat a bullet wound. I limp down the stairs out into the fresh air and light the ciggie. I walk to the corner, where the bus stop is, and lean against it, looking like a suave motherfucker.

I suck down on the ciggie and ask myself the obvious question.

What would Columbo do next?

Well, I guess he would look for the most famous person he can see, then keep pestering them like a day-old fart until they crack and tell him how they did it. Then he probably takes that dog home and does something nasty. That's not going to help me very much. But what advice would he give me?

Follow the money.

That's what they say, isn't it?

That'll do, pig.

Sixteen
Lambert

Rab's body moved easier than Lambert expected. It was loose and pliable. Maybe it was the drugs in the corpse's system, or maybe it was simply the first time Lambert had dealt with a corpse so fresh. Usually he came to them later, once someone else had done this bit and tried to hide it.

He tipped half a bag of lime over the body. He'd read somewhere that it helped cover the smell, and quite a few of the murder scenes he'd attended had seen bodies coated in the stuff. Next he wrapped it in a plastic sheet, a shower curtain he'd bought from Asda the day before, and then bound the bundle with elastic tow rope. He tipped the other half of the lime over the bundle and then laid the wooden board on top.

That would do.

For now, anyway. The harder work would come later. Bodies didn't start to smell as quickly as people thought; nobody passed by this lock-up, and Anderson would be fine there for up to three or four days, if need be. Once the heat had died down. In both senses.

Lambert locked the door behind him and climbed into the car. He pulled out his phone to make a call, then caught himself and realised what he was doing. He reached over to the glovebox and slipped out another phone, one that wasn't in his name, and punched in a number he knew by heart. He waited while it dialled and then clicked over to voicemail. He hadn't been expecting an answer; nobody ever picked up the call live, but the messages were always listened to.

'I had to change the plan,' he said. 'Our guest had to check out ahead of schedule. You know where I am.'

Lambert ended the call and pulled the car out onto the road, making sure to wait until there was no traffic to see where he'd come from.

Bed was calling.

Killing someone, Lambert had discovered, will jack a person up quite high. The blood and endorphins had been racing around his system, better than any drug he'd tried. But the comedown was equally harsh, and his energy levels drained on the drive home, with nothing but the monotonous routine of stop, start, indicate, pause, go.

He took the motorway, figuring the constant traffic and over-taking would force him to stay awake. Home was only a ten-minute drive down this stretch of road. He lived in Paisley, a large town a few miles out from Glasgow, and he made it back without falling asleep at the wheel.

The estate where he lived with Jess was modern, a small collection of two-storey terraced buildings set back from the high street, and he saw there was already a car in his driveway as he approached. An obscenely shiny BMW.

His father-in-law.

Joe McLean. A business owner and developer. He'd been a cop, a long time ago, before his investments in land had started to pay off. Now he made a good living from buying and selling land and investing in new property developments. McLean climbed out of the car and waved at Lambert as he pulled up, all big gestures and broad smiles, playing the happy family. He stepped forward to slap Lambert on the shoulder.

'Andy, son, how you doing?'

'Tired.'

Lambert walked on past him to the front door and stepped inside the house, leaving the door open for McLean. In the living room, which was very clean and very white, the two cats glanced at the newcomers. One was black, which always set off a latent superstitious streak in Lambert; the other was ginger and shaped like a rugby ball. But it wasn't feeding time, so they settled back down to sleep. Once inside, the mood of both men changed.

McLean's smile dropped away.

'Jesus fucking Christ.' His tone dropped below freezing. 'My golf caddy is a better fucking criminal than you. We agreed how this was going to go. We made a deal with everyone.'

'We did. I changed the plan. I had to—there are too many people looking for him. It's going to be difficult to get rid of him dead. It would have been impossible to hold onto him alive.'

'Is that right?' McLean paced the room, Lambert stepping out of his way. 'And you're the expert on all of this now, are you? Are you going to be the one who explains to the washer lady why we changed the deal? You going to talk to Gilbert?'

Lambert slumped onto the sofa. The cats hissed and ran through to the kitchen. This hadn't been how he'd planned on spending the day. It wasn't how he'd planned on spending his life, for that matter. He was at the end of a run of five midnight shifts, and it was his weekend now. He just wanted it all to go away.

'Look, Joe,' Lambert said, unable to keep the sulk out of his voice, 'there was no option. I was protecting you. Us. The law might come looking for him now, and I don't want them sniffing around either one of us. What would that do to Jess? There's a solicitor firm in the city too, and they've hired a PI to find him.'

'A PI? We still have those?' McLean didn't see the problem. 'Fine. I've dealt with them before. We threaten him or drop him in the Clyde.'

'It's *her* not *him*. Samantha Ireland. Sam. Jim's daughter.'

'Jim Ireland's girl, is that right? That's interesting. I thought she was going to university, wanted to get away from Glasgow and move somewhere hip.'

'Aye, that was the plan. Dropped out of uni when Jim got sick. She's only doing the job because she thinks it's what her old man would want, keep the family business going.'

'There's a son too, right? Philip?'

'Aye, he works with her. Drives her around, goes into scary places with her. He's a big lad, looks like a bouncer crossed with an ape. They might be useful, though. You wanted to find out if anyone else knew what we were doing, right? Well, if Sam and Philip are going round shaking trees, then they might draw a few people out into the open.'

'Which "open" would that be, Andy? You've seen too many films. All that's going to happen if we let her go around asking questions is that she'll lead people right to us. She needs to shut up.'

'I'll make sure it doesn't come to that.'

McLean stopped pacing and peered down at Lambert. He'd spotted something in the tone of voice. 'You fucking her? You cheating on Jess? Is that what I can smell on you?'

In truth Lambert didn't know whether it was sex or death that he smelled of most.

'No, I, just—look. We both knew Jim, right? We both owe him. Rab had it coming—he was in the game. Sam doesn't, and that's not a line I want to cross. All she's done so far is get threatened in the Pit. I'll make sure she doesn't get in too deep.'

'Maybe.' McLean nodded. 'Maybe. We do owe her old man. We should try and keep to that. You know who else is owed? Me.' He waved at the room around him. 'Who gave you this? Who paid for you to marry my daughter? I've taken a chance on you, and you keep fucking up.'

'I know. I know. I'm sorry.'

'Aye, I'm starting to think *sorry* is my name, the amount of times I hear it said to me.' He took a deep breath and made a show of smoothing out his coat, calming down. 'We'll try it your way. Keep an eye on Jim's daughter; see if we can play it nice on this one. You mentioned the Pit—how is Murdo looking?'

'He might be a problem. He's already asking questions.'

'Did Rab give up anything else last night?'

'No. He just kept babbling. Too many drugs, I think. He kept crying and apologising, over and over. He called out Mackie's name a lot—you know his nephew? Well, that's his name. I've met him a couple of times, not the brightest spark.'

McLean stared at a photo for a long silent moment. A snap from the wedding, Lambert and Jess smiling, on a children's climbing frame. Lambert couldn't read the expression in his father-in-law's face.

'His nephew is going to have to go as well. Can't have him running round.'

'Who will we get to do it?' Lambert said.

McLean turned to him, his face blank. 'You, bozo. Start cleaning up this mess.'

Lambert yawned and ran a hand through his hair. He felt his shoulders sag. McLean opened his coat and fished around in a large pocket stitched into the lining. He pulled out a clear plastic bag and tossed it at Lambert.

Lambert caught it with both hands and looked down at the pills inside the bag.

Speed.

McLean spoke without any trace of humour. 'Sleep when you're dead.'

Seventeen

One of the advantages of being a cop was that Big Brother was on Lambert's side. He had him on speed dial. He had Mackie's full name and address within minutes, along with his full grisly history.

Malcolm Jack Mackie lived in Govanhill. It made perfect sense. He'd served time for slicing up his high school sweetheart, and Govanhill was the murder capital of Scotland. It was a small part of town just south of the river. The slum landlords were out of control in Govanhill, with run-down houses and crowded tenements. The council turned a blind eye to the conditions so it could shove immigrants into those tenements and forget about them. There had been more murders in those few crowded streets than anywhere else in the country.

Just last year Lambert had picked up a case in which a driver had been dragged from his car and stabbed to death, all for the crime of running an amber light at a crossing. Even driving *through* Govanhill on the way somewhere else could be a dangerous game. It was only a matter of time, at the present rate, before even the police refused to go there.

Mackie lived in a four-storey tenement on Bowman Street, nestled between a bookie's and an old cobbled lane that ran along the back of his building. Lambert took a walk down the lane before doing anything else, to get a good sense of the area. It helped to see if anyone was likely to care before you committed a bunch of crimes. He had to step over a mattress that smelled of piss and a bin that had been tipped on its side, sending the litter and dog shit across the cobbles. There was a low metal railing separating the yard of Mackie's building from the alley, and it allowed Lambert to get a good look at the back windows. Mackie lived on the third floor, and the windows were dark, even with the sun beating down. They gave off a sense of emptiness. *Work in this job long enough,* Lambert thought, *and you learn to spot it.* There was nobody inside.

He walked round to the front door and pressed the buzzer for Mackie's flat. It was easy to spot; it was the one with 'fuck off' written on the nameplate. When there was no answer, which he'd known there wouldn't be, he started pressing the other buttons until he got a response. He announced he was *polis*, and the door buzzed open.

Lambert climbed to the third floor. Another advantage of being a cop was learning how to break into places. A rookie police officer will attend enough B&E calls in his first year of uniform to learn how to break into pretty much anywhere. The outer storm door was closed, but nobody ever locked the mortice. The second lock was a simple latch, and all that took was a credit card and a few seconds. Lambert pulled on a pair of gloves and worked his way through the storm door. The inner door was going to be more of a problem. It was a simple enough Yale lock, but it was deep in the wood, with no easy way to get at it. The door was flush against the frame, and the lock looked new. A large frosted pane of glass covered the top half of the door, casting a dim light inside, and that was going to be the quickest way in. Lambert shrugged out of his coat and held it up over the glass, then punched the lower left corner, near to where the lock was. The sound was unmistakable, like stepping on broken glass on a hard floor, but it was muted enough for him to get away with it. He knocked a few remaining jagged bits of glass from the edge and reached through the fresh hole to open the door from the inside.

The door swung inwards and banged heavily on the wall. He stood in the doorway for a moment, listening for any reaction. Inside he found the light switch. The sunlight wasn't penetrating the curtains, and the flat was cast in darkness until Lambert started flipping the switches. The walls were painted brown, which may well have been covering other stains, and there was a hardwood floor. The ceilings were very high. In the hands of anyone other than Mackie, this could have been a nice place.

There were five doors leading off the empty hallway, and Lambert took them one at a time. The first one, beside the front door, led to a cupboard piled high with junk. Coats, boxes, bags, a ladder. All the essentials.

The next door opened onto a large bedroom. The heavy curtains were on the far side, with a metal bed in the centre covered in sheets that hadn't seen clean in a few months. Clothes were piled around the floor. Lambert knelt down and found shed carcasses of carpet beetle larvae ground into the floor. In a pile next to the bed were handwritten letters. Each one was addressed to 'Jenny T', whom Lambert guessed was Jennifer Towler, the girl Mackie had cut up when he was younger. The letters varied in age; some were old and faded, with the ink nearly gone, and some were fresh.

Next was the living room. It was clean and sparse, with just a sofa, a chair, a large TV on a table and a shelving unit piled with DVDs. Lambert checked out the collection to judge Mackie's taste; it was an odd mix of 80s action and Disney cartoons. On the floor beside the sofa was a *Columbo* box set, a stack of comics and a few empty cigarette packs.

The kitchen was a mess. A holy shit pile of a mess. There were plates stacked on every surface, with dust and mould, and a lot of full bin bags heaped by the door. Empty pizza cartons were scattered across the floor. There was a sickly sweet smell in the air, and Lambert found an air freshener plugged in at an electrical socket.

So, Mackie was the kind of person to go to a shop, buy the freshener plug-in, bring it home and set it up, all rather than carry a few bin bags down a flight of stairs. Lambert suspected he wasn't dealing with a criminal mastermind.

Next to the kitchen was the bathroom, which was actually quite clean. There was a little dirt on the shower tiles, and a build-up of toothpaste in the sink around the plug, but nothing that couldn't be sorted with five spare minutes and a cloth.

'What kind of person lives in a place like this?' Lambert asked out loud, mimicking the old TV show catchphrase. Someone who spends more time in the pub than in his own flat. He sleeps here, watches DVDs and only steps into the kitchen to dump plates and takeaway cartons.

Then he found Mackie's stash.

Back in the living room, Lambert had noticed that the DVDs were pushed right to the front of the shelves, with space in behind them. He went through, shelf by shelf, until he found bags and bottles of pills.

Cocaine.

Speed.

Medication.

Some of the bottles were genuine prescriptions, with Mackie's real name printed on them. Others had a woman's name. Lambert pocketed the speed and coke. They might come in handy later on. There would have been more money to be made in taking the medication, but he didn't like to mess around with it unless he knew for sure what it was.

He lowered himself onto the sofa and stretched like a cat, tabbing another speed to keep the sleep away, though it would be a while before it kicked in. It wasn't a great batch.

Sit there and wait?

Go out and find him?

The easiest thing was to deal with Mackie here. Clearly he lived alone and didn't get visitors; there would be no problems. But he didn't know when Mackie would come home or what state he'd be in. If Lambert went on the hunt, he could corner him, pick and choose the time and place.

Then what?

Look at you, he thought to himself, *pretending you're a pro at this. Pretending to be some kind of cool bagman, rather than a coward, too scared to stand up to your father-in-law.*

His phone rang, the unlisted one.

As soon as he accepted the call, he heard someone talking fast on the other end. He recognised the voice but still waited to hear the introduction.

'It's Gilbert,' the voice said. 'We have a problem. I need to talk to you about Mackie.'

What were the odds?

Eighteen

Lambert drove back towards the city and parked up in Carlton Place on the south bank of the Clyde. Stretching from there to the north side of the river was a suspension footbridge. He walked across it, pausing for a second to look down at the brown oily surface of the water and check he wasn't being watched.

At the other side he turned and walked down some concrete steps to stand beneath the base of the bridge. It was a perfect spot for discreet meetings, out of sight from the road on both sides of the river. People walking along the path could see you, but you could also see them coming.

Gilbert Neil was waiting there, leaning on the low railing and staring out at the water, doing the same trick Lambert had done on the bridge. He knew Lambert was approaching but played it cool, letting him get close and then speaking without turning around.

'It's really shite, isn't it,' he said. 'The river? People all over the world know the name of it. The Clyde. It's in books and songs, old poems. They think it's old and romantic. Then they come to look at it and find nothing but a brown sludge.'

'Aye.' Lambert leant in beside him. 'But it's *our* brown sludge.'

'You Weegies. You love the city—until it's time to burn part of it down.'

'It's ours to burn. Listen, Gil, there's been a change of plan. Rab had to go ahead of schedule.'

If Gilbert was angry, he didn't show it. He was a practical man. He lived his life by dealing with complications as they arose, and this was just another one to sort out.

'The washer lady will be pissed off,' he said. 'That's not how we agreed to play it. But we have other issues too. Mackie's been asking around for Rab. The Pit, Gaz, me—he's working his way through everybody.'

'You've spoken to Murdo? Does he know anything?'

'Not yet. He called me to give the heads-up on Mackie, but he also asked if I'd seen Rab. He's starting to wonder. He's just a beaten-down old fuck, so we can deal with him when he figures it out, but it's bigger than that. Too many loose ends; people are starting to talk.'

'You mentioned Gaz. Gary Fraser?'

'Aye. Mackie went to him because Rab did, last night not long before we grabbed him. He'd asked Gaz for a loan of sixty Gs, so it's not connected; but it brings Gaz into the circle, someone else who might start wondering what's going on.'

'And why is Mackie asking? What's tipped him off so fast?'

'Someone tried to kill him last night.' Gilbert finally turned to face Lambert. 'Two hit men. In the house on Copland Road. To be honest, I'd assumed it was you or Joe who ordered it.' When Lambert shook his head, Gilbert went on. 'The Venture Brothers.'

'Venture Brothers?'

Gilbert smiled. 'Look, I know it's a stupid name, and you know it's a stupid name. But just in case there's a little old lady out there going by the name of Mrs Venture, and now grieving her two boys, I think we should stay quiet on the name, stupid or not.'

'Grieving?'

'Well, like I say, they *tried* to kill Mackie. He killed them instead. Two people, with guns, and he was naked and unarmed, and he won. Shot one with his own gun, beat the other. He took a bullet in the leg, and it didn't even slow him down. A hooker died too, some Polish lassie, only been in the country five minutes.'

Gilbert turned and walked towards the brick wall at the base of the bridge, further out of sight from passers-by. Lambert followed.

'So, who the hell ordered the hit?' Lambert asked.

Gilbert stayed silent. No point answering if he didn't know. They both stayed quiet while a couple of joggers moved by. One was in good shape, pumping away at a steady pace; the other was slow and fat, wobbling from side to side and breathing like a heart attack on legs. Then a cyclist came in the other direction, coasting along the path while checking something on his phone. Lambert almost flagged him down on principle. There was a junkie-looking guy further up the path, heading their way, but he had no real speed to his walk and exhibited the lazy shakes of a guy who got too high once and never came down again.

'I'm not really sure we should care,' said Gilbert. 'We've got bigger issues to worry about, and if someone wants to take out Mackie, they're helping us. All we need to figure out is how to deal with the mess. I've not told the washer lady about it yet, trying to keep it locked down. I've got Nick ready to go in and clean it up as soon as we know which way you want to play it.'

'It brought Mackie into play. He's asking around now because of that, and I'm guessing he knows his uncle has gone, maybe went to the flat and saw the mess we made of the dog?'

'Yup.'

'Great. There's someone else too. The PI. Sam Ireland. Yeah, Jim's girl. She's been hired by some law firm to deliver papers to

Rab, so between Mackie and Sam we now have to get the loose ends tied up a lot quicker.'

'Here, you, big man.' The junkie had drawn level with them. He stepped in close to Gilbert. Lambert could feel his bad breath. 'Giz yer fuckin' wallet or I'll fuckin' chib ye.'

Lambert and Gilbert both turned to give the guy the stink eye and said in unison, 'Fuck off.'

Junkie hadn't factored this into his plan. In truth, he didn't look like he'd factored much of anything into his plan. He nodded and looked down at his feet, but didn't move. After a few seconds, Lambert and Gilbert both decided to ignore that he was still there, and fell back into conversation.

'It would be good for business if we could clean all this up with no further damage,' said Gilbert. 'But to be honest, I have a bad feeling.'

Before Lambert could answer, the junkie started again.

'I'm fuckin' serious, by the way. See this?' He hand was in the front pocket of his tracksuit jacket. He raised it, with his finger pointed through the material, trying to make it look like a gun. 'Stand and deliver, pal.'

'Is that finger loaded?' Gilbert said. Then, with more venom, 'Look, we said no. Fuck off.'

Lambert pulled his wallet out of his inside pocket. The junkie's eyes lit up for a second until Lambert opened it and showed his warrant card. Lambert then waved the guy away and turned back to Gilbert.

The junkie started to walk off, then stopped.

''Scuse me, pal.' He was all polite. Like he hadn't tried to hold them up with a finger. 'Could I borrow a pound for the bus home?'

Lambert rolled his eyes and fished some change out of his pocket, throwing it at the guy. The money hit the ground and rolled off in different directions, sending the junkie crawling after each coin.

When Lambert turned back to start the conversation again, Gilbert was staring into his eyes. 'You don't look right. What're you on—speed? Coke? Are we going to have a problem here?'

Lambert stepped in close, getting in Gilbert's face.

'You putting this mess onto me, making out I'm the liability? Whole reason we had to move on Rab so fast was because—'

'I know. I know.' Gilbert put his hands out in a peacekeeping gesture. 'I started it. Let's not get each other wound up over this. We've made a mess, but we can get it fixed. What do you want to do about the Copland Road house? I've been sitting on it in case you wanted to use it. Maybe we let the cops find it, and you can use that as a way to get Mackie, arrest him for the crime.'

'Too messy, too reliant on chance.' Lambert shook his head. He was playing it cool but wanted to smile—he'd found a way to push the dirty work onto someone else. 'Last thing we want is to bring the law anywhere near a member of Rab's family right now. We just want Mackie dead, no fuss. You got someone can do that?'

'Sure. Easy. Once we find him. Won't take long, he's making so much noise. What about you, what you doing?'

'I need to keep watch of Sam, make sure she stays out of trouble. We can honour the thing with her dad as long as she stays away. I took a peek at the legal papers too. I might go see the law firm and find out what their angle is.'

Lambert started walking away.

'Get some sleep,' Gilbert called after him.

'I'll sleep when I'm dead.'

Nineteen
Sam

I took a quick shower and changed into my running gear. I was all about the branding for most of my running kit. Black Adidas Sequencials shorts and a Supernova racer bra from the same company, usually in purple. It was really too hot for a top, but I'd never been comfortable running without one—I felt exposed. I wore a light zip hoodie over the bra. The only break in my style was my trainers. I'd tried all manner of expensive running shoes, even the fashionable natural ones that everyone raved about, but I kept coming back to the same broken-down old pair that I'd first started running in when I went to university.

Running hadn't been part of my life until then. I caught the bug in my first semester and bought the cheapest and ugliest pair of trainers I could find, so that I wouldn't feel like I'd lost anything if I only ever went for the one run. Even now, almost four years later, these were the only pair I felt comfortable in. And they were almost falling apart. I'd decided it was insurance. There was no way any harm could come to me while I was out running, because it would be just too embarrassing to be found dead in them.

I was going to need a shower again once I was done, so the first one wasn't really necessary, but it was better than running around with the smell of sex all over me. I crossed the road to Glasgow Green and then started running. Jogging at first, taking a slow pace, easing into it alongside the river. I'd not been running often enough lately, and I could feel it. My thighs were tight and I was very aware of what my arms were doing, that self-consciousness that dropped away when you ran often. First I tried to ignore my arms. Then I tried pumping them in time with my stride, but then what did you do with your hands?

Open fist? Closed fist? Tom Cruise-style karate chop?

I got impatient and stepped up the pace, heading into a full run, and pushed myself more than I should have. I lasted half a mile before my lungs were screaming for me to stop. I leant against the railing beside the river and coughed, letting my body take its revenge on me before I sucked in some air and started calming down.

Why was I angry?

Was it because of Andy?

I knew he was married and also that he was trouble.

But I'd been hung over, and then high from what had happened at the Pit, all those juices pumping around my body. There are two ways to work all of that out of my system: sex or running. I'd decided on both. Andy was okay at it. He was selfish and a bit repetitive, but he liked to go slow. He was one of those guys who must have watched a lot of porn before ever having sex, so he talked all the way through like a porno star. While you were with him you were his *baby*, and everything needed to be *oh yeah, just like that*. Fortunately, given his age, it must have been porn from the late eighties and early nineties, so his expectations weren't as way off as younger guys. He wasn't expecting silicone and bits that didn't move. He wasn't expecting a million and one different positions on the way to getting the job done. But I'd been with Andy before, so

89

that wouldn't be enough to get me pissed at myself. Plus, I'd left the flat without my keys, and if you wanted someone to break and enter for you, a cop was usually the best option.

It was because of amateur hour at the Pit.

I couldn't imagine my father had ever pulled such a stupid stunt. But then, maybe he hadn't needed backup. When he walked into a room, people took notice.

With my head cleared, I started running again. I did it the right way this time, keeping my pace even, pushing myself just enough to feel it. I ran around the opposite edge of the Green, turning back towards my flat and passing by Doulton Fountain as a busload of tourists piled out to take pictures.

Back at the flat I stripped down and took another quick shower. My third of the day. Maybe I was going for a record. I got dressed in a shirt and jeans and started planning what to do next. Enough of the amateur crap. I was going to do this one right.

I still had Rab's address on the folded piece of paper Andy had given me. First I needed to put in the research. I knew of Rab by reputation, but that wasn't good enough. My dad always said a reputation is only enough to get you a beating. I booted up the computer and typed Rab Anderson into the search engine. The hits threatened to overload my tired old machine. I flicked through news stories and book reviews, a few video features on local websites and a whole lot of grainy videos on YouTube: people meeting him in bars and at book signings; or Rab drunk in bars, singing football songs. Then I saw the most recent news hits. Rab had signed a new book deal. The book was to be called *Firestarter* and was going out through a national publisher, not one of the smaller local ones he'd been with before. This seemed to be major news, and there were a lot of blogs arguing that his books shouldn't be published and that criminals shouldn't be allowed to profit from their past, through film and book deals. I checked the news report again, and it gave the book's publication date as being this month, but when I checked Amazon I saw the pre-order option for the book had no date listed.

Interesting.

Had Rab missed the deadline?

I fished in my bag for the legal paperwork that Fiona Hunter had given me. I wouldn't have opened it myself, but since the asshole at the Pit had already done it, I felt entitled to read through the documents. The language was very dry, very prim and proper. Very legal. But I'd seen enough overdue payment demands in my life to know what this was. Rab hadn't delivered on the contract, and the publisher wanted the advance back.

And if Rab no longer had the money, it was no surprise he was playing hard to get.

I dialled Phil's number. It went through to voicemail. I hung up without leaving a message and dialled again. Same result. On the third attempt he answered with a sound like a bear being pulled out of a coal mine.

'You went back to bed, didn't you?'

'Well, I was up late last night.' There was defensiveness in his voice. 'There was a wrestling pay-per-view.'

'Who won?'

'Nobody good.'

I was going to ask if it was anyone I'd heard of, but I hadn't watched wrestling since I was in my teens. And even then, I only knew the names of about three of them. I got straight to the point. 'Suit up, Robin. I need a ride.'

'You know, I don't think Robin gets to drive the Batmobile. He's a kid—it's against the law even in America.'

'I'm not well versed in this, but I'm pretty sure Batman is a vigilante, not known for obeying the law in his giant bat costume. He throws a boy into the middle of fights with psychopaths and killers—I'm sure he'll let him behind the wheel of a car.'

'True, okay. But even still. It's Batman who drives the car. And Robin's a girl right now, I think, so you know what that means?'

'Not happening.'

'Come on. You want this ride or not?'

I hissed at him down the phone. Then gave in. 'Okay, Batman, come pick me up.'

Click.

Twenty

Phil pulled up outside my flat in his Ford Fiesta. He looked like he'd dressed in a hurry, with tracksuit bottoms and a large grey hoodie that was too heavy for the summer heat, but that's how he always dressed. His face was creased with tiredness and a few days' worth of stubble, and I could smell pot in the car.

Rab's flat was in Cessnock, only a few minutes away from the Pit. After giving Phil the address, I leant back in the seat and waited for the snark, but it didn't come. He sat in silence as he drove across the bridge and along Ballater Street.

'Are you awake?' I asked after a long pause.

'I'm being silent and moody, like Batman.'

'Right.'

'Also I'm very tired, did I mention that?'

'Okay.'

'So what's going on? Is this the job you took from the hotshot lawyers?'

'Right. I'm looking for Rab Anderson. Yes, that one. Seems like he took a large advance from a publisher for a true crime book and never delivered the work, so they want him to stump up the book or the cash.'

'Shit. I hope they're paying good, because Anderson isn't someone I'd really want to find.'

'They are. Anyway. Andy gave me a lead, Rab's address, so that's where we're going now.'

He thought this over for a moment. 'So we turn up, ring the doorbell, say, "Hiya, Rab," deliver the papers, then fuck off?'

There was no way it'd be that easy.

'Hopefully, yes.'

We turned off Paisley Road West and onto Clifford Street, which looked like it ran to both cheap and expensive. Some of the red-brick tenement buildings were worn and faded, with overgrown yards and water-damaged doors. Others looked well kept, with newly fitted windows and clean curtains. The address on the slip of paper took me to a building that looked halfway between the two extremes. It was lived in but tidy. We parked directly outside, pulling in at a space at the kerb, and Phil led the way to the front door.

None of the names on the buzzer said 'Anderson', but the second one down was listed simply as 'R.A.'. I guess you had to know what you were looking for. Phil pressed it, and we both waited. There was no reply.

'Ach, well,' Phil called out in a fake cheery voice, 'he's not in. Let's go.'

My dad used to say that being a cop was great for learning how to break into a building, but then he'd start telling stories about the past, and I'd stop listening. I wished I'd let him teach me a few tricks. Instead, I pressed the buzzer again, then started pressing all the other buttons in turn.

On the third attempt I got a reply, someone who sounded bored and tired, like they didn't give a shit who I was as long as I wasn't looking for them. Tenement flats are great that way. So easy to get into as long as you present no hassle to the person you're asking to let you in. I told the bored voice that I had a book delivery for Rab, and the door opened with an electronic buzz.

I climbed the stairs slowly, trying not to make enough noise to entice anyone out to check on me, and trod quietly past the door of the person who had let me in. Phil was less discreet, carrying the weight that he did. On the top floor we found Anderson's flat, again with the simple initials on the sign next to the bell. The storm doors were open, showing just the main front door inside, a dark wooden job with a large pane of frosted glass in the top half.

The key was in the lock.

I rang the doorbell and waited for a moment as a precaution. Then I took a grip on the key and turned it slowly, trying to ease the mechanism open. The door swung inwards on a squeaky hinge.

The hall was simple and mostly bare. Dull green walls and laminate floor, with a radiator on the far wall, a telephone stand and four doors. The smell of bleach and soap covered male sweat and the unmistakable aroma of dog. The four doors led to a bedroom, a living room, a kitchen and a bathroom. The rooms were all pretty sparse. In the kitchen I found an open tin of dog food, half of the contents still inside, on the countertop next to the sink. The sink had a few traces of recent use. There was a pre-cooked curry defrosting in the fridge, alongside a six-pack of Tennent's.

On the wall in the living room was a picture I assumed showed Anderson's dog, a dopey-looking black and tan boxer with his knob hanging out. The dog was nowhere to be found. I noticed the mail piled up on the kitchen counter. Everyone dumps their letters somewhere, usually in the same spot each day. Over time a pile builds up that glares at you until you throw it all out, unread. But this pile was all addressed somewhere else, to a property nearby in Ibrox. Most of the letters had Anderson's name on them, but a few were addressed to a woman, Neda Tenac.

There was a pile of loose change and another set of keys next to the mail. If Anderson was anything like me, then this was the spot he would empty his pockets out when he got home. So did he go out for the night without his keys and cash? I rattled the keys in my hand.

'Why would he leave his keys in the door?' Phil sounded nervous.

'I went out without my keys today. Shit happens.' I said. 'But that's not the question.'

'What is?'

'You ever read the Sherlock Holmes story about the dog that didn't bark in the night-time? Rab has a dog. You can smell it, though someone has been doing a lot of cleaning in here with bleach.'

'I don't like the sound of that.'

I nodded. 'Someone's trying hard to make-believe like everything's normal, but all they're doing is reminding us about the dog that isn't barking. No dog, Rab's keys, even this loose change. Something's not right here.' I felt a hunch building and decided to let myself follow through on it, be a real detective. 'I don't think Rab is going to turn up.'

'You think someone's hurt his dog?'

'I think someone's hurt *him*.'

'Uh, Sam, all you're doing is making a good case for us not being here. Either the cops will be coming, or the people who did Rab will be coming. We need to be somewhere else.'

He was right.

The obvious thing to do was to call Andy. The grown-up thing to do was to call Andy. The thing my dad would probably have done was to call Andy. But I was sick of running away, sick of asking for help. At least not before having something solid to hand over, an actual case that everyone would say I made. I picked up the letters with the other address on them. It was in Copland Road, only a few minutes away.

'You're right,' I said. 'Let's be there, instead.'

Twenty-One

Copland Road was across from Ibrox subway station. One side of the road was lined with council-run tenements that had been recently renovated, but as we drove down the road, counting the house numbers, we found ourselves looking at the other side of the street, with tired-looking houses and overgrown front yards. It was only a couple of minutes' walk from the football stadium and not far from one of the busiest stretches of motorway in the UK, but it might as well have been in another world.

I half-expected tumbleweed to blow by.

'I don't like this,' Phil said.

'You don't like anything.'

The address off the letter was halfway down the road, a faded white house sandwiched between two boarded-up buildings. The house's small front yard was hidden by an overgrown hedge. The hedge would give us some privacy, but the path was a short one, with the front door only a few feet from the pavement, and two of us would draw attention.

'Stay in the car,' I said to Phil. 'I'll be less noticeable on my own. Keep your phone out, and I'll call if I need anything.'

'There's a shop back there.' He nodded further down the opposite side of the road. 'I'll go get some chocolate. Want anything?'

'Cornetto?'

I shut the car door and walked down the short path to the house. I pressed the doorbell and waited, but there was no answer. Once I was sure there was nobody in, I pulled out the keys I'd lifted from Anderson's flat and started trying them in the door.

On the fourth key the tumbler turned and clicked, and I swung the heavy wooden door inwards. The hallway was dark and cold, and the silence of an empty house echoed around me. The inside was better kept than the outside, but still wouldn't win any awards. The walls were painted a deep burgundy colour, and light fittings were halfway up, with dimmer switches below them. The wooden floor had been sanded and varnished, and my footsteps sounded out around me.

Why would Anderson live in a tenement flat if he had a house?

Doors lined the left-hand side of the hallway, and I could see a staircase at the end and another door, presumably to the kitchen if this house followed the normal design. I opened the first door, to what I assumed would be the front living room, and found a bedroom. The room itself was painted a dull blue. It had a sink in the corner, a small coffee table, and a double bed. That was it; there was nothing else that marked it out as a home. I pulled the door shut and tried the next one, and found an almost identical bedroom. The only difference was that the walls were a dull red.

I turned and climbed the stairs, each one creaking slightly as I went. At the top I found that the first door I came to was a cramped bathroom, and the door next to it was another bland bedroom.

I stood on the landing and sucked my lower lip for a moment while I thought.

What the hell was I doing here?

Why was every room a bed—*Ah*.

'Well done, Captain Obvious,' I told myself. 'You've found a knocking shop.'

I decided to try one last door, just because it was closed and I was curious, and promised myself I'd leave after that and go find Andy. I placed my hand on the doorknob of the front bedroom but paused. The hairs on the back of my neck stood up, and something felt wrong. I pushed the door open and stepped inside. The room was decorated with the same blue paint as the first one I'd seen downstairs. There was the same double bed and even the same coffee table.

But someone had gone to the trouble of adding a few extra features.

There was blood splashed across the wall above the bed, and the sink was full of something clotted and fleshy. The sheets had been pulled back from the mattress, and a damp red stain ran diagonally across it and down to the floor.

Something horrible had gone down here. I dreaded to think what the person who lost all of that blood was looking like, or where they were. I pulled out my phone, and my fingers hovered over the buttons, inching towards Andy's number.

Get the hell out.

Get the hell out.

I heard someone whistling out in the street, a lilting tune that I didn't place at first. 'Teddy Bears' Picnic.' Something about that tune had always scared me, and now wasn't the time to be hearing it. I headed for the top of the stairs but then froze.

The whistling was getting closer.

The tune paused for a second, and I heard someone messing with keys. Then the front door opened, and I wasn't alone in the house any more.

I stepped back into the bedroom and pushed the door shut as quietly as I could, easing up on the door handle so that it shut with a muffled click. I stared at the phone in my hands again and started to dial Phil's number. The whistling had started again and I could hear someone taking slow, heavy steps on the staircase. I heard whoever it was step into the bathroom, then the plastic sound of a bucket being placed in the bath, followed by running water. I looked around me at the blood and realised it was clean-up time. I became conscious of how loud the phone was in my hand as it rang out, and how long Phil was taking to answer it. I killed the call.

The whistling came towards me down the hallway.

I looked around the room. The bed was too low to get under, the windows were nailed shut, and there were no closets or cupboards.

I listened to the tune and watched the door handle turn.

PART THREE

'What scares me is that you're starting to enjoy this.'

—*Phil*

Twenty-Two
Sam

The handle turned and the door started to open. I had seconds to think of something, but my mind was blank. Did I mention I was new to all of this? I wondered how big the guy on the other side of the door was, and if I stood a chance. What weight could I throw into a punch? I'd never done it before. I could probably outrun whoever it was, but that was only useful if I was on the other side of him.

Time stood still.

The front doorbell rang.

You could be in a strange house anywhere in the world, and yet you'd instantly recognise that sound. The door in front of me stopped opening. I heard a grunt, and then the floorboards creaked as whoever was on the other side shifted their weight, deciding whether to go and answer the front door. Then the bell rang again. There was another grunt, and the person on the other side walked down the hallway, and soon I heard the creak of the stairs.

I opened the door and stepped out onto the landing, placing my feet at the sides, hoping to avoid the creaking floorboards. There were two buckets and a mop placed by the door. One of the buckets was full of warm bleached water; the other was dry but full of sponges. I made it to the top of the stairs and peered down, but I couldn't see the front door. The angle of the staircase kept it out of sight.

I heard the door open, and then I heard Phil's voice.

'Hello, sir.' He spoke loudly, doing a half-arsed impression of Brian Blessed. 'Could I talk to you please about our Lord and Saviour Jesus Christ?'

There was a grunt, the same one that had just been inches away from me, and a hoarse eastern European voice said, 'Eh? No. I thank you.'

I heard the door start to close, but something stopped it. I imagined it was Phil's foot. 'Really, sir, He loves you. He loves me too, though He's not so much a fan of what I get up to in my spare time.'

This caught the man's attention.

'Excuse?' the foreign voice said. 'No understand.'

'No, well, me neither. Seems the all-powerful Creator of all things only likes one kind of sex between two set groups of people. Anything else is strictly forbidden. Unless it's done by very old people in the Bible. Those old guys can marry as many people as they like and have sex with anybody. The rest of us? Nope.'

The foreign voice stammered again, trying to figure out what the hell was going on.

Phil didn't give him time. 'Seems he's quite a forgetful god, all told. Or maybe just clumsy. He lets people like me who want to be with other men run around. He lets herbs that we've decided are illegal grow in the ground, because I guess God doesn't know nature like we do. And he also can't ever seem to keep hold of money. He's always asking for a loan.'

'Well—'

I tested the weight of the top step, but I felt it starting to flex, and pulled back before I risked it creaking. There was no way to make it down without being noticed, and I would still be on the wrong side of the cleaner. I pulled out my phone and sent Phil a text.

Keep him talking.

'See, what I wonder, sir'—Phil kept on going—'is why he would want it all that way? And then—oh, excuse me, I'm sorry, this might be important. No, it was nothing. My apologies. So where were we? Oh yes, have you ever seen *Transformers: The Movie*? I mean the cartoon from the eighties, not the recent one. It has a great soundtrack. All cheesy power ballads and soft metal. Do you like metal?'

I stepped into the bathroom. The door was open, and I thought closing it might draw attention when the cleaner came back up. He might remember the way he'd left it. I stepped into the bath and pulled the shower curtain over a little, keeping me from sight. I sent Phil another text telling him to go and get the car engine running.

'Tell me, sir, where do you stand on zombies? Should they run? Do you prefer the shuffling ones? I bet you're a modernist, am I right? You like the new ones, the ones who run. I have this film idea, about the zombie Olympics and—hang on again; sorry.' I heard him checking his phone a second time. 'Well, it's been a pleasure talking to you, sir. You have a nice day.'

'Uh, yes.'

The door closed. Footsteps came back towards the stairs, then climbed them. I held my breath and waited. The cleaner stopped outside the bathroom door. Had he heard something? Could he see me? He didn't move. I realised holding my breath had been a stupid idea, because I would make noise when I drew in another. I kept my mouth closed and held in what little air I had.

There was a soft laugh. 'Zombie Olympics.'

Then the cleaner walked on towards the end room.

I heard a car starting up out in the street. I leant around the shower curtain and peered down the hallway. The cleaner was short and square, facing away from me as he knelt down in the bloody room, inspecting the far wall. I stepped out of the bath silently and then took a step forward.

The floor creaked.

The cleaner turned and saw me. His skin was olive coloured, with creases across his face and white stubble on a large jaw. His eyes grew wide as he looked at me. Then he rose to his feet, lifting a hammer in his right hand.

A hammer? Who carries a hammer?

Fuck it.

I ran. I took the stairs three at a time, then skipped the whole bottom half. I landed awkwardly and stumbled, but stayed upright and made it to the front door. I fumbled with the latch, which was stiff and needed to be oiled. I heard the cleaner on the stairs. He was heavier and slower than me, and not willing to try the jump. It gave me the seconds I needed. I got the door opened and ran out into the street. Phil had already pulled away from the kerb and was idling the car in the middle of the road, with the passenger door open. I slid into the seat and pulled the door shut. The cleaner barrelled out of the house towards us, with his hammer raised.

Phil didn't need me to tell him to drive.

'Nice of you to wake up,' I said.

Twenty-Three

'You know what scares me the most?' Phil looked over at me and waited for me to ask what it was. When I waited him out, he put his eyes back on the road and carried on. 'What scares me is that you're starting to enjoy this.'

I smiled.

He was right.

My heart was pumping, and the adrenalin was revving my engine like crack cocaine. Was this why Daddy used to do it? I'd only ever seen him at the end of the day, tired and worn out. I'd grown up convinced that it was only the idea of holding the family together that had kept him going, but was it the thrill of the chase?

'Is it that obvious?'

'You're practically bouncing in your seat. What happened back there?'

'No, you first. How did you know to ring the bell?'

'Not much to tell, to be honest. I came back from the shop and saw him going in the front door. You weren't in the car. I guessed it was better to assume you needed help than to assume you didn't, and I rang the doorbell. I hoped an actual plan would come along once I started talking.'

'You talked an epic amount of pish, by the way.'

'Is that a criticism or a compliment?'

'It's a thank-you.'

He smiled. We drove through Govan, or what was left of it that arsonists hadn't torched. We took the Clyde tunnel, taking us across the river. There was a game we'd played ever since we were children, of holding our breath as we went through the tunnel. Phil could never make it, but the advantage of having runner's lungs was that I could last longer. He punched me playfully on the shoulder as we came out the other end, his way of admitting defeat.

'Your turn,' he said. 'What happened back there?'

'I'm not really sure, but whatever it was, it wasn't good. There's a room covered in blood, and I'm not sure there would have been much left in the person who lost it. I think someone's been killed.'

'By that guy?'

'Maybe. Or by a customer. Might even be Rab's blood, but that feels too easy, like too much of a coincidence. That place was a brothel. And I think Rab was the person who ran it, him and some woman named Neda Tenac.'

'Neda who?'

'It's a name that was on some of the mail at Rab's flat. Some of it was the Copland Road address.'

'So there's a room full of blood in a brothel and a psycho with a hammer. You know what I think we should do?'

'Call the police?'

'Call the fucking police.'

We passed a phone box, and I waved for Phil to pull over. Usually if I called something in to the police, I did it through Andy, but he would be in bed asleep. I wanted there to be no way to trace it back to my own phone. I dialled 999 and gave them the CliffsNotes version of what they would find at the house, which was pretty much the only version I had. House, blood, man with hammer, hang up. I had another call to make, but this one would be a charged call, and I couldn't find my purse. When did I last have it? Had I left it at the flat?

Ooooooooooooh shit.

I didn't remember seeing it since the Pit. If they hadn't given it to Andy, they might have my address. Great. Another thing to add to the list of problems I didn't have when I woke up this morning. It could wait, though. I was still buzzing with the excitement, the hunt for answers. I could get used to this.

I slipped back into the car and pulled out my mobile. Then I dialled one of my saved numbers and waited the few seconds it took for an answer.

'Greetings, Crowther & Co. How may I be of assistance?'

'Hi, Alexei.'

'Sam.' I could hear his smile down the phone. 'Did you like my telephone voice?'

'I did. It was very professional. And another new word—you'll be reading Shakespeare in no time. Is Fran in?'

'Indeed so; bear with me.'

The line went quiet save for an occasional beep to tell me I was on hold.

'Sam.' The beeping ended, and Fran Montgomery boomed down the line at me. 'I'm hoping that you're calling about the divorce case I gave you and not because you're still looking for Rab Anderson. I've heard his name a lot today. Seems like there's a lot of people on his trail.'

I hadn't told Fran that I was looking for Rab. People must be talking. It was good to know I wasn't paranoid. I really was in the eye of a storm.

'Still looking. I've rattled a few cages. Andy Lambert had to bail me out of a mess in Cessnock. I'm getting a bad feeling, Fran. I was in Rab's flat, and it felt like someone had cleaned it up a little too much, got rid of evidence. I'm not sure Rab is going to be found. I've got one lead left. Have you heard of someone named Neda Tenac? I'd like to track her down—well, I assume it's a woman.'

'Aye. She's a woman of sorts, I guess. Listen, Sam, when you say Rab's not going to be found—'

'I think maybe he's dead.'

'That's what I thought you were going to say. Sam, I've worked with Tenac. She's old school, and scary. The wrong word, and she might hurt you.' Fran rarely let something like that slip. He kept his opinions on his clients to himself, so it carried extra weight when he shared them. 'This is going to sound patronising, and I'm sorry, but I think you should walk away now. Tenac isn't safe. None of these people are safe. This isn't a case for you.'

His apology only made me feel more patronised. I was sick of being written off, sick of being patted on the head and underestimated. Mostly it was out of guilt, because I'd spent so long doing it to myself.

'Apology accepted, Fran, but I'm not twelve, and I'm not just playing at this. It's my job now, and I'm going to get it done. Where will I find her?'

There was a pause on the line. I could almost hear the face he must have been pulling, the tussle that went on before he spoke. 'She runs the laundrette on High Street, across from McChuills.'

'I know the place.'

McChuills was a fun little pub. It was often full of Celtic fans and had a pirate flag flying outside. I'd been in there a few times, but I doubted the welcome was going to be as warm across the road in the laundrette.

'Sam, it's great to see you so fired up. Your dad would be proud of you. But if you keep talking to these people, you're not going to like some of the answers.'

He hung up, maybe to avoid my next question.

What did he mean?

Twenty-Four

Back in my father's time, High Street had been a dangerous place, all crumbling tenements and football pubs. The kind of place he didn't like me going to on my own. Another street that had suffered from accidental fires.

More recently, though, it had been taken over by the creeping gentrification that was changing the face of my hometown. The university had built new student accommodation on one side of the street, which had brought in supermarkets and fast food shops to cater for the kids.

The opposite side of the street was still living in the past, with a row of tenements and small businesses on the ground floor all along the block: a grotto, a hairdresser's, two cafés, two eastern European food shops, and a laundrette.

The laundrette perched at the far end of the block. The front was mostly taken up by windows with green and white paint around the frames. Mesh covered the windows, protecting the glass from a non-existent riot. The windows were large, and even with the mesh covering they still let a lot of light into the interior. I told Phil to stay outside and keep an eye on me through the window; he would only come in if I stepped out of sight.

I pushed through the door. The inside was full of noise, with washing machines lining one wall and tumble dryers lining the opposite side. The back wall was taken up by hangers full of clothes. There was the smell of damp and warm clothes in the air, and the line of machines were creating a loud rumble on either side of me. A short woman stepped from between the hangers to greet me. She was solid and square, with a face that was set into a scowl. Her age could have been anywhere between fifty and a million.

'How I help?' she asked.

Her accent was heavy, and she seemed to think about every word.

'I'm looking for Neda Tenac?'

She looked me up and down, tilting her head back as she did. 'Who ask?'

'My name's Sam. I'd like to talk about Rab Anderson.'

'I not know Neda—or he.'

I pulled one of the letters I'd lifted at Rab's flat out of my pocket. One that had Tenac's name and address. I handed it to her. Her expression changed while she read it—lightening a little, with the hint of a smile tugging at the edges of her lips.

'Well, you're good, aren't you?' Her accent shifted. It still carried traces of eastern Europe, but now it showed signs of having been corrupted and eased by a long time living in Glasgow. She took on a conspiratorial tone. 'The gorilla outside, hen, is he with you?'

'He is.'

'Wise. A lot of people're looking for Rab today. Most of them scarier than you.'

I needed to think on my feet. I decided to play dumb, to still be thinking Rab was alive. 'I'm working for his publisher. We want to talk to him about his manuscript, but I can't find him.'

'Girl, are you a bad liar. Everyone who's looking for Rab? They're all talking. You're the private investigator, Sam Ireland, and you're looking for him for a solicitor who works in the town. You lie to me again, and I may be not so nice to you.'

That last line carried all manner of threat and promise. I started to notice how large her hands were, calluses on her knuckles like an old boxer.

'You're right. I'm the PI.' I hit back with something I knew, revealing one of my cards to up the ante. 'The house in Copland Road—you work for Rab, or do the two of you run it together?'

Despite the heat from the dryers, I felt the temperature drop in the space between us. Her eyes grew hard. 'Tread lightly, hen. You're getting noticed today and not by people who are nice or patient. You're getting noticed by people like me, and it's a mistake you only get to make once. This isn't your world.'

That was the last time I was going to be patted on the head. I went all in.

'You don't know what my world is, but I know yours. You and Rab, you work together. You sell women's bodies, and you pocket the money. I've already tipped off the police about Copland Road and all the blood they're going to find in the bedroom. If you really want to play the game of who has the scariest friends in town, then how about I call them again and tell them you run the house?'

She blinked. Lost her grip on the situation for a moment. I'd thrown something at her that she hadn't known before.

'Blood?'

I pushed the advantage with a smirk. 'Oh, you've not been told? Someone's donated a lot of blood to the walls in the front bedroom.

Enough to make me think the person who lost it isn't walking around any more. Someone was trying to clean up the mess, but the cops will be there by now, and he's probably in custody.'

'Describe this man.'

'Like a smaller version of the Easter Island statues. Accent like yours. Carries a hammer, but he's not as cute as Thor.'

'Nick,' she said, more to herself than me. She nodded. 'One of Gilbert's boys. For them to keep that secret is bad. It means a lot of people, everyone who was there, is staying silent.'

'Why would they force you out?'

I asked that without knowing what she actually *did*, but I figured one thing at a time.

'Business. People are useful until they're not. They are scary until they're not. When they're not,' she stuck her bottom lip out and nodded her head to the side, like she was talking about a bad game from her favourite sports team, 'they go away.'

'Has Rab gone away?'

'Maybe.'

'But you do work with him?'

She looked like I'd spat in her face. 'Again you push. All the insults. I wouldn't work with Rab. He's an arsehole. Or was.' She enjoyed her own joke. 'We share interest in one house. It's the one he wouldn't sell to me. He wanted to keep a stake in Copland Road, but we do not work together.'

'So what do you do?'

'I keep peace. This town? Divided. It's like *West Side Story* here. People want to talk, negotiate, they come to me. I give safe ground to both sides. Nobody moves on anyone when they're with me.'

'And the house in Copland Road?'

'Okay, I also run a few whores. There's a recession on—you have to take profit where you get it. Losing that house will be unfortunate, but it will be a minor problem. Even better, you've just given me this letter, shown me a few other tracks I need to cover. Rab has a way of annoying people. He causes too much trouble, and it was always a matter of time before he annoyed the wrong person.'

I became very aware of my own position. I was closer to Tenac than the door, and she was telling me things she had no reason to share. Was she going to let me walk out the door knowing all of this? The thrill of the chase gave way to a very basic fear, and for the first time since leaving Copland Road, I thought about my own well-being.

Tenac peered into my eyes. She clapped her hands. Two other women stepped out from behind the clothes. They looked like Tenac's older sisters, wiry and hard. Both carried knives.

'Know this, hen. I'm answering your questions because I think maybe I like you and because you've given me important information. But it could have gone the other way, and if you ever cross me, or if you tell any of this to the cops, it can still go that way. And I would know if you talked to the cops.'

I swallowed and nodded.

'There are people in this city not to be messed with. People I won't mess with. Rab, he forgot that; he's gone. I think maybe these people have decided to ignore their deal with me, so I have to go and make some phone calls now. So this is the favour I'm going to do for you. Walk away now. You've done enough. You've done more than any of the other lazy investigators would have done. They would have walked away at the mention of Rab's name. Your fancy lawyers probably came to you because you didn't know enough to say no. They used you, so use them.'

'What do you mean?'

'I have to do your job for you now? Write a report, pad it out, tell a few lies and make it look like you're owed some expenses. Go and get paid for the day's work. Then go home, forget the names you've heard today and hope they forget you. Do what your father would have done.'

It was her turn to throw something new at me. My mouth opened before I found the words to fill it. 'You know him?'

'Of course. That's why I let you talk to me.'

Twenty-Five

I visited my dad most days around 4.00 p.m. This time I was half an hour late. Everyone I spoke to on the job always talked about him in the past tense, as if he was already dead. I think for most people it was easier that way. It meant they could seal off Jim Ireland as a memory and not think of him as he was now.

I hated to admit it, but I was jealous of them. I didn't get that luxury. I was going to be with him until the end, and I didn't know if I would be able to remember him the way he used to be, by the time that end came. And today had only made it worse. Tenac knew my dad. Was that what Fran had meant? Was that why Andy had tried to warn me off the case? I don't know why it came as a shock. Dad was a cop in the city for over a decade, and then he worked as a private investigator through an era when Glasgow was a lot rougher than it is now. It was only natural he'd be on terms with some of the darker and scarier people. It made sense that he'd had to walk away from a few interesting cases to save his own skin.

But no matter how much my brain rationalised it, my heart felt a little broken. Nobody wanted to see their parents as human beings, not really. We wanted them to be the same mythical figures they used to be when we were kids, as solid and dependable. Human beings were the people we met out in real life, at our jobs and our pubs and our nightclubs. But parents? They were archetypes. They were meant to stay the same.

Phil drove me out to the home but didn't want to come in. He hated seeing our father as he was now, and he'd been scared of hospitals and care homes ever since he was a child. Some people coped with it, some didn't. I never judged him for it, but it was something else I was jealous of. He got to choose when to play family and when to ignore obligations. I didn't have that choice in me. I had to hold the family together in whatever broken form it took.

The home was in an old private school building on the road to Paisley. It had been heavily modified and rebuilt over the years, but the front still looked like a budget version of a castle, with large brown bricks and turrets on the corners. Inside it smelled like any other care home. Air freshener and humidity covered the smell of old age, medicine and surrender. There was a constant babble of televisions in the background, and the nurses always did their best to smile and not let the stress show. The fees were expensive, but it was better than any of the NHS places we'd looked at, and they'd been willing to negotiate on the figures.

Dad was watching a rerun of a Jim Garner film, laughing along at the bits he remembered. He looked up at me blankly for a second as I pulled a chair alongside him. His cheeks were paler than the last time I'd visited, and stretched tighter across his jawline. He was slowing sinking into himself. Not the superhero he'd been when I was younger: Jim Ireland, policeman turned private investigator. Square jaw and fast mouth.

'My daughter used to love this one,' he said to me with a wink.
'Aye, she told me.'
His eyes lit up. 'Is she here?'
'She will be in a minute.'

He nodded and leant back in his chair, eyes drifting back to the screen. The film went to the ad break, and he leant in to talk to me again. There was a different look in his eyes this time. The lights were on again. 'Where's your brother?'

'He's working.'

'Uh-huh, sat out in the car, right? Aye. That's okay; I could never stand these places either. Still can't, but on the bright side I'm only here part of the time.' He chuckled. I didn't. I couldn't find the humour. 'How's the office?' he asked.

Closed.

Working from home.

Bailiffs are scum.

'Aye, it's doing good. We'll take you out for a visit one of these days, let you sit behind your desk again, if you want.'

He smiled, happy again. 'Aye, aye. Can we do that?'

'Course. I'll talk to the nurses about it. You still giving them hell?'

He practically glowed. 'There's a new one, think she's got a thing for me. Always tells me off during the bath. Aye, it's the old Ireland charm—I've still got it. How about you—got a man yet?'

'Too busy at work.'

He gave me another of his intense looks, the ones that told me he knew I was leaving things out and that he knew what they were. He'd always had that ability and not just with me. If it hadn't been for old prejudices running deep, he would have gone all the way in the police force. Maybe he'd still be well.

'Daddy, I'm working a big one. Maybe *the* big one. Get the family name in the paper again; let the world see it like in the old days. You remember Rab Anderson? I was hired to find him, but it looks like he's been taken out, like a proper gang hit or something.' I looked into his eyes when he didn't answer, and I wasn't sure if he was in there. I didn't want to think about that, so I carried on.

'There's some guy called Gilbert Neil—he's involved—and I was just talking to Neda Tenac. Says she knows you. She said you'd have dropped the case, left it alone. I don't believe that.'

The film started again, and he focused back on the screen. A couple of minutes went by, and he turned to me. 'My daughter used to love this one,' he said.

I kissed him on the forehead. He smiled and nodded at me. 'Careful, it's not bath time.'

I told him I'd see him later and left before he saw me upset.

We didn't talk for most of the drive back. Phil never asked how Dad was. He didn't want the truth, and he didn't want to turn me into a liar. It wasn't until we were on the edge of the city that he asked where I wanted to go.

'Home,' I said.

I didn't say any more. I was ready to take Tenac's advice, although I didn't want to say so out loud. I could file the report, collect a day's pay. Rab was dead, and I had no need to find him. But now I had another itch, one that was even more dangerous. Dad's case files were in my spare room. I wanted to go through them, see what connections he had to Tenac and Anderson. Even worse, see if Gilbert Neil's name came up. How many times had my dad walked away?

Andy had known my dad. Worked with him a few times. He'd have a good take on what I needed to know. I sent him a text asking for a call when he was awake.

Phil dropped me at the door and honked the horn as he pulled away. I fumbled in my bag for the keys and let myself in. I opened the door to the living room.

The old man from the Pit was sitting on my sofa, smiling at me.

The dinner lady from hell was beside the door, waiting for me.

She raised a gun and waggled it, motioning me further into the room.

It was only as I shut the door behind me that I remembered my missing purse.

'Hi, Sam,' the old man said. 'There's someone who wants to talk to you.'

Twenty-Six
Lambert

Lambert remembered the name of the law firm, but not the address. He hadn't been able to look at the documents for long before handing them back to Sam. It only took a quick Internet search on his phone to find the location. He left the car where it was and walked. Driving into the city could be hell, especially once you were locked into the one-way system at the heart of the grid, and it was only twenty minutes on foot.

The firm was in one of the large grey stone buildings that never went out of fashion for rich people. Lambert got a bad feeling straight away, and the directory inside the main door confirmed it: the firm had the building to themselves. Nobody got a building like that to themselves any more. Even the larger firms shared with telecommunications companies and debt collectors.

These guys had too much money.

It raised questions.

The reception was painted in light shades of brown and tan, cut through with black. The furniture matched the colour scheme, and Lambert had to wonder which came first. Was the room decorated to match the furniture, or was the furniture made to order? There was no scent of any kind in the reception. Not even a nice one. It takes epic amounts of money to remove every single smell from a space used by humans.

Sam didn't have as much experience with the larger firms, Lambert knew. She was used to rubbing shoulders with the storefront companies down on Saltmarket. She wouldn't have noticed all the warning signs when she'd visited the office that morning, but Lambert couldn't fail to miss them.

Companies with a bit of money liked to show off. They would have their own magazine in the reception area, or personalised music. Companies that wanted to seem like they had money would buy stupid features that served no use, like a piano or a metal moose head. This was a different league. This was a company that had a lot of money and no need to show it off. They were in total control of their own space.

They were dangerous.

Behind the reception desk was a young woman dressed in sleek, dark clothes. She smiled up at Lambert and asked how she could help. He thought of telling her to run for her life, but instead flashed his warrant card and asked to see the boss.

'Which one?' She didn't look at the ID. She kept her eyes and smile locked on Lambert. 'Doug or Fiona?'

'Both.'

'Take a seat.'

She picked up a black phone that Lambert hadn't even noticed was there and started having a hushed conversation. Lambert headed over to the large sofa and perched on the edge of it. He didn't want to relax into the cushions in case it was a trap and he would never want to get up again. He caught the first smell since he walked in, and realised it was himself. Sweat, lime and sex. An unpleasant mix of everything he'd been through that day. His embarrassment was kept away by a swell of pride; he was stinking up an area that someone had paid a fortune to sterilise.

He checked his watch, and it was quarter past three. Where was the day going? Jess would be home from work soon, and today she was expecting him to be there, asleep.

The receptionist put down the phone. 'Doug will see you now,' she said without raising her voice. She didn't need to, since they were the only two people there. 'I'll show you the way.'

She led Lambert through a glass door and up a flight of stairs to the top floor. He was out of breath by the time they reached the top, but didn't want the receptionist to see that. He sucked in some air and tried to offer her a cool smile.

'Right through there.' She pointed at the frosted glass door ahead of them and then headed back downstairs without a breath or hair out of place.

Lambert knocked on the door and then walked straight through without waiting. Being a cop gave certain permissions. One of the perks of the job. The office was decorated the same as the reception, but with more glass. There were black and white pictures of the local area on the walls, each taken with a different arty lens, and a large glass desk in the centre with nothing on it. Not even a few stray coffee cup stains.

Behind the desk was a young man. Lambert sized him up as he walked over, and the man stood up to meet him. The best description Lambert could think of was 'pretty'. He was thin and groomed, with elfin cheekbones and short blond hair that was left longer at the front to allow for a gelled quiff. It was almost translucent, and light shone through it from the window behind him.

When he spoke it was with a polished accent that carried a Scots brogue wrapped around a bland Englishness. 'Hello, Officer. My name's Doug—Doug Simpson. How can I help?'

He offered his hand and Lambert took it. The grip was firm, not what Lambert had expected, and he realised he'd already made certain assumptions about Simpson. He'd have to watch that—it was the quickest way to set yourself up for a fall. There was also no attempt at a Masonic handshake, which was unusual in this city.

'Your partner not here?'

'Fiona's in a meeting with a client at the moment, and it's not one she could duck out of. She'll join us shortly when she's finished, if you still have questions. This is official business, I take it?'

Lambert skipped by the answer to that one. He wanted to let Simpson's own assumptions work in his favour.

'I need to ask you about Rab Anderson.'

'Rab Anderson?' Simpson stared back at Lambert. He'd not blinked yet. 'I don't believe he's a client of ours. Tell me again, is this part of an official investigation?'

The game had started. Simpson was fishing to see how much Lambert knew. Lambert, in turn, was trying to weigh up Simpson. Who was going to make the first move? Who was going to crack first?

'When it comes to Anderson,' Lambert said, spinning a half-truth, 'it's always official business.'

That was only part of a lie. There was an open file on Anderson. At any given moment there was someone working a case that linked to him. It was just that Lambert wasn't one of them.

'I see.' Simpson smiled and offered his first blink. 'So you have the paperwork to back this up?'

'Call my superior, if you want. I'll give you his number.'

Lambert didn't get a chance to see if his bluff would be called.

The door opened behind him, and a young woman stepped in. Lambert turned in his seat to look at her. This had to be the 'rich lady' Sam had mentioned. She was dressed in clothes that probably cost more than Lambert's car, and walked with a steel and poise that Simpson lacked. Lambert rose to shake her hand, but she stepped past him, coolly ignoring his presence and making him feel like a naughty little boy. No wonder Sam was impressed.

'You look like you've had a hard day,' Fiona Hunter said, finally turning her clear blue eyes to Lambert. 'Department working you hard?'

Ouch.

'Mr Lambert was asking about Rab Anderson,' Simpson said.

'Oh?' She sat on the edge of the desk, her foot kicking out at the air. 'What about him?'

'I understand you're handling a case involving Anderson. I'd like to know what it relates to. It might tie into a matter I'm investigating.'

Hunter nodded. 'Let's say, hypothetically, that I hired someone this morning to find Anderson and serve papers on him. The only way you could know this is if that person told you or if you read the papers that were to be served. That would be unfortunate for you, on a professional integrity level, but even more so for the person I hired. We take a poor view of that kind of confidence breach.'

Shit. Lambert had dropped Sam right in it. He'd not been thinking straight since last night—mistake after mistake. Things kept escalating.

'I can assure you,' he said, not sounding the least bit assuring, 'that any information I have has come through the correct channels.'

'I am assured.' Her voice carried a wicked edge. Simpson smirked behind her. 'But stop assuming we are fools. If the police had an official matter to raise with us, they wouldn't send someone high on drugs and smelling like a pub. Now, if you're here on your own, maybe acting on a side interest, that would be a different matter.'

Lambert decided to run with it. At least, he told himself, it was a decision, because that let him pretend he was still in a position to be making them. There was only one person controlling this conversation.

'Go on,' he said.

'If we keep the hypothetical conversation going for a moment, let's pretend we both have ulterior motives in this. Maybe, for the sake of a good story, you're a rogue cop who's tied up in some of the same dodgy deals as Mr Anderson. Let's also say that we hired a young private investigator to find Mr Anderson as a way of smoking out some of the people involved in these deals.'

'That would be a clever way of doing it.'

'Thank you. If we had done such a thing, it would have been my idea. Now, imagine that both of those things are true. I'd suggest that the rogue cop in question was not exactly the top of the chain of command in this little enterprise.'

Lambert stayed silent. There was nothing to gain by answering, and a hell of a lot to lose. He stared up at Hunter and waited until it was clear that he wasn't going to fill the silence. Then he thought of something, a way of clawing back some control.

'And if this were all true,' he said, 'would you be the kind of people to have ordered a hit on Anderson's nephew, maybe as another way of drawing people out?'

Lambert smiled and sat in silence again. He made a show of checking his watch, timing the silence, and felt good.

'Nice touch,' Hunter said. 'Maybe I underestimated you. But the point stands.'

'What we're saying'—Simpson leant forward—'is that we don't want to be sitting here talking to the monkey. We want the organ grinder.'

'And of course'—Hunter's tone changed, becoming warm and conspiratorial, the good cop now in the routine—'we'd pay the monkey a hell of a lot more than peanuts.'

Twenty-Seven

Lambert stood out on the street, trying to decide his next move. He felt the pavement moving beneath his feet. It had been moving ever since the whole thing had started, a couple of stray conversations leading to murder, kidnapping, and now who knew what. The promise of payment held his interest. This was a firm with serious money, and maybe a taste of that would be enough to get him and Jess out from under his father-in-law's thumb. That could be between him and the lawyers.

Lambert headed back down the street. On the walk down to the river, he pulled out the unlisted phone and dialled the number.

'New problem. Looks like there's an extra player. Someone else is asking about Rab, and they have real money. They're asking to meet you, though they don't know your name yet. Only a matter of time. Give me a call when you get this. I think you should meet them.'

Jess would be home by the time he got there. He didn't want to run the risk of her catching him before he'd had a shower, a chance to be more human and get rid of the grime of the day.

A pit stop. That's what they'd always called it on the job. Changing your tyres and refilling your oil before you headed home. For some it was necessary after the grind of the job, getting rid of the smells that came from crime scenes, drug dens and dead bodies. A way to keep a clear line between work and home life. For others it carried a smuttier meaning, a chance to get rid of the smell of booze or sex before heading back to the husband or wife.

For Lambert, today, it was a mix of both.

He drove to his office in the police building on Stewart Street. It was a square modern building, decorated with blue glass in case people were in any doubt that it was a police station. He had an assortment of clothes in his locker. A pair of jeans, a spare work shirt, two odd socks, and the jacket off a cheap suit he'd bought from Asda. There were no briefs or boxers, but he could live with a little freedom. He left both phones charging in the power sockets beneath his desk and hit the shower.

Stepping under the warm water felt like heaven. It scoured his face and back and wiped away the sweat. He pulled off the bandage from his hand and let the water clean the wound beneath. It looked nasty. The skin had pulled back around the cut, and was pale and waxy. There was a blue tint to the very edge of the skin, maybe an infection. He'd get it looked at once everything else was fixed. The warmth of the shower brought on the tiredness in waves, and Lambert was yawning heavily by the time he stepped out and towelled down. Back at his desk he checked his emails and messages.

Fuck.

Callum had written up the floater as a suspicious death. That would mean an investigation. It would mean Lambert having to put in hours on a murder case, and might even mean he'd have to come in and work on his two days off.

He pulled the first aid kit from his desk drawer and started redressing the wound, and dialled Callum's office number while he worked.

'McGalty,' Callum said. 'How can I—'

'Why?'

'Oh, hi, Andy. I thought you were clocked o—'

'Suspicious?'

'Have you read my preliminary report?'

'This better be good.'

'Okay. Your cadaver is a Mr Rupert Prentice Venture. Yes, the name caught me too. It's an unusual one. He's from England, and the records still have him living down there, so it's strange for him to wash up in the Clyde.'

Venture was the name Gilbert had given for the two dead fraternal hit men. That only left the mystery as to where the second one had been dumped. Gilbert had said one of them had been shot and the other beaten to death.

Callum continued. 'Now, this is the interesting part. Our man has no water in his lungs. Not a significant amount, anyway. He wasn't drawing in breath when he went in the water.'

'He didn't drown.'

'No. It looks like he was beaten to death, though it could also be consistent with falling from a great height or maybe even certain kinds of traffic accidents, though none were reported yesterday, I believe.'

'Okay, so he didn't kill himself.'

'Well, it's possible he did, but he did it by beating himself to death before jumping in the river.'

'Was that a joke?'

'I thought I'd make an effort. Enjoy the investigation.'

The line cleared.

Okay. It was a murder investigation. What's more, Lambert knew who'd done it. And now he also had an idea of why the

Venture Brothers had been sent after Mackie in the first place. But he'd need to steer the case away from Mackie. Get Mackie a frame-up, or maybe just let the case go cold and take a hit on his closure rate.

Twenty-Eight

The unregistered phone rang as Lambert walked up the path to his house. He put the phone to his ear and answered, huddling in on himself as if it created a soundproof barrier to the world.

'We've found Mackie,' Gilbert said.

'Where?'

'Hospital. Don't know the details, but he got picked up in town, taken to A&E. They're stitching him up now.'

'Cops?'

'Two on the scene. One is Cummings—my two guys recognise him. There's a woman with him, younger, Asian. We don't know her.'

'It'll be Perera—she's his new partner. They're good.' Subtext: They can't be bought. 'They can't take him in.'

'What do you want us to do?'

'You know. He's a sitting duck right now. Don't wait. First chance, take him out of the game.'

Lambert hung up and unlocked his front door, stepping into the porch to kick off his shoes. He could hear the radio in the kitchen as he walked in the front door. Usually Jess would be singing along, unless he was in bed, but she was silent. He listened out for the sound of her working, maybe tidying something away, doing some washing or preparing a meal, but there were no other noises.

Maybe she thought he was already in bed. Maybe she hadn't checked.

He opened the door to the living room and saw Jess sitting on the sofa, waiting for him. She looked nervous. She had subtle, pixie-like features that looked great most of the time, but they didn't lend themselves to worry. Her small frame was hunched in on itself.

'We need to talk,' she said, with eyes that looked a little wet.

There was something in her expression that made the bottom drop out of Lambert's world. It was the same look she'd had the night her mother died, and the time one of the children from her school had gone missing. The same look she'd had the first time she thought he was cheating on her, when she'd found another woman's underwear in the dirty laundry.

Had she heard him on the phone?

Had she figured it out?

He ran off a mental inventory of all the other things she might be upset about, and then started figuring out which version of the truth to tell and how to blame it all on Joe. She patted the space on the sofa beside her, and Lambert sat down slowly.

He put his hand on her thigh and squeezed.

'What's wrong with your hand?' Jess noticed the bandage. 'You get hurt?'

'Got bit by a dog on a call-out. It's nothing.'

'A bite? You should get it looked at, get a tetanus shot.'

Lambert nodded, pulled his hand back towards him.

'I've been late for a while now,' Jess said.

'At work?' He spoke before his brain engaged, and before the words were done leaving his mouth, he knew what she actually meant. 'Oh.'

She squeezed his good hand.

'I've taken the test,' she said. 'I'm pregnant.'

Twenty-Nine
Mackie

Whut?

Takes me a minute to figure it out.

I'm lying on my back, on top of a bed. It's flat and hard, like my old prison bunk but less comfortable. There's a pillow beneath my head that feels like a dead cat. Someone's nicked my trackie bottoms and trainers. I'm just wearing a T-shirt and pants. There's the smell of bleach or medicine in the air. Maybe both. Oh, my leg has been bandaged. I'm in a hospital. I'm in one of those wards where they put you in a bed and pull a curtain around you, hide you away. I can hear people being treated either side of me, behind the curtain. I try to move but I feel woozy and light-headed, maybe drunk.

How did I get here?

Well, that's a deep question, I suppose.

But no, really, *how?*

One minute I'm in Glasgow, walking down a street. Then I blink, and it's all beeping and bright lights being shone in my eyes and people asking if I know where I am.

'I'm in fuck off and leave me alone,' I say. 'You know the place?'

I close my eyes again, and when I open them, it seems to be a long time later and I'm in here. I stay still and try to remember details.

Follow the money. That's what I'd said. Except I didn't know where the trail started. Gaz had the cash, but it wasn't going to be getting up and moving for me to follow. That left Gilbert, right? He said he didn't know what the cash was for, but he's a lying cunt, so I figured he'd know what was going on. I stood at the bus stop at the end of Drury Street and waited.

People were starting to look at me funny—I remember that. I gave them the evil eye, and they moved on. I saw Gilbert step out of the pub and turn the other way, heading towards West Nile Street. I gave him a head start and then followed. My leg didn't want to take my weight, so the going was slow, but I kept at it. I felt like I was slowing down with each step, and I shivered a couple of times, cold in the middle of a heatwave. Gilbert walked down Mitchell Street, past all the nice titty clubs, and then crossed over to St Enoch's. I thought maybe he was going to go down into the subway station, but he kept going, heading towards the Clyde.

Then my world wobbled a little bit, and I felt sick. I bent down to throw up, and that's the last I remember.

While I'm trying to think of more, the doctor steps into the cubicle. He looks like a real doctor. He's older than me and has a beard, black-rimmed glasses and a white coat. All doctors should look like this. He's wearing a name badge that says 'Gilmour'.

'How you doing, son?'

'I don't know, Doc; you tell me.'

He smiles. I like that. If you need a quack, it should be one with a sense of humour.

'Well, I'd say you got shot and lost a lot of blood.'

'How much?'

'A lot. The bullet didn't hit anything major, but you don't look to me like you've been giving it a chance to close up and seal itself, so you've been slowly bleeding out.'

'I've been a bit busy, aye. Shit to do, you know?'

'Aye, okay. Well, you're meant to have around eight pints in you, give or take. I'd say you've lost about three. Any more than that and you'd be dead. You collapsed when your body went into shock. That's when your body starts to shut down to protect you, like going on standby. I'm surprised you lasted as long as you did.'

'Three pints? For real? So I'll never have a full load again?'

He smiles, tries to hide a laugh but fails.

'Son, your body makes blood all the time. It tops you back up. We've given you a transfusion, a couple of pints, so you're probably feeling a little weird right now—drunk maybe?'

'A little, aye.'

'Okay.' He pats my leg. It doesn't hurt. 'The wound has been dressed and treated. As long as you rest it up, it won't reopen. And you need to sleep, give your body a chance to catch up. You're still around a pint down, but that's nothing to worry about as long as you rest and take plenty of fluids.'

'Like beer?'

He laughs again. 'Like water, son.'

'Well, I drink it like water.'

He pauses before he steps out through the curtain. Then pretends to remember something that I bet he's been working towards the whole time. 'By the way,' he says, 'there are some police officers here who want to talk to you.'

He steps to one side and holds the curtain open, and two cops walk in. Neither of them looks like Columbo. One is a fella, tall and bald, with a beer belly and glasses. The other is a lassie, about my age and Asian. She keeps in shape but doesn't look like she's enjoying it. Baldy looks a bit like Bert from Sesame Street, but the lassie looks nothing like Ernie.

Baldy flashes me an ID.

'Hello, Malcolm.' I hate being called that. I bet he knows. 'Remember me?'

'You all look alike.'

'Aye. Well, I remember you, son. I remember all the blood on you the day we booked you in for what you did to that girl. My name's DI Cummings. This is DS Perera. Do you know why we're here?'

'Well now, that's a bit of a deep question, isn't it? I was just saying that to myself.'

Perera steps in closer to me and takes a look at my bandaged leg, then leans to peer in my eyes. She holds that position until I blink, trying to make me uncomfortable. It works.

'He's not concussed, John,' she says as she moves back beside Baldy. 'He's just being a dick.'

'Aye, I figured him for that. Malcolm Mackie. Mack the knife. I know all about you, son. I was in the station the day they pulled you in for cutting up that wee lassie. Saw you covered in blood, crying and screaming, saying how sorry you were.' He turns to his partner. 'You know, you can butcher someone now and not even serve a full term in prison.'

I can feel myself shrinking inside my own head, back to being a teenager. I don't like to think about what happened. It makes me cry, and nobody wants to see that. I wish Beth was here with some pills—they stop me thinking about it. It's the only thing I like about them.

'You came in wearing a bullet hole,' Perera says. 'So now we have a problem.'

'See,' Cummings speaks again—they've rehearsed this—'we haven't had any reports of gun crime in the city this week. None at all. That's good for us, makes us look like we know what we're doing. But now you're here with a bullet wound, and that means we have a gun crime with no gun and no bullet.'

'Sucks to be you, big man.'

They share a look, and then Perera nods and steps out through the curtain. Cummings leans in closer and does the trick of staring into my eyes for a second, but that's something I'm only going to fall for once. This fucker tried using Jenny against me. He's getting nothing.

'You have a think,' he says. 'We're going for a coffee. When we get back, we're going to interview you about a crime. You can either be the victim and give us some names and limp out of here on your own, or you can be the criminal and be led out in cuffs. It's entirely up to you.'

He turns and leaves.

He doesn't look back to see me giving him the finger.

Thirty

Next through the curtain is Beth. She's dressed up all professional-like, with her hair pulled back. She's carrying a clipboard, and she looks hot. I think I should tell her.

'You look hot,' I say.

She fumbles over her greeting for a second and almost blushes. *That's my girl.*

She looks down at the clipboard and takes a second to get professional again.

'You lost three pints? Mack, you could have died.'

'Aye, the doctor said that.'

'What happened?'

'I'm not really sure. Well, I got shot, but you already knew that bit.'

She steps in close, looking all worried, and puts her finger to her lips. Am I talking too loud? Probably. I'm all drowsy and don't really know what I'm doing, so I could be shouting.

'Sorry.' I lower my voice. I think. 'So, I was following Gilbert in town, but then I collapsed. Next thing I know I'm here, all better.

They've stitched me up and put a whole lot of blood in me. It feels funny, like taking drugs.'

'The cops are outside,' she says. 'I've talked my way in as your doctor, but I won't be able to stop them. The nurses here had to report the bullet wound, and you're going to be arrested.'

'Aye, I figured that bit out all by me own self.'

'They won't be able to keep you in. There's no proof. No bullet—just a wound that the doctors have already fixed up. They'll keep you just long enough to try and scare you into saying something about what happened—then they can hold you for longer.'

'Bollocks to that.' I sit up and swing my legs off the edge of the bed. 'I'm getting out of here.'

My leg goes all funny, like the worst case of pins and needles in history, and I go all light-headed. It passes quickly, but it isn't fun. Beth steps close to me and puts her hands on my shoulders, pressing me back down.

'Take this,' she says, handing me a pill.

'I'm sick of those.'

'Just this once, Mack, don't do the wrong thing. This'll calm you down, slow your heart a bit, and you think better when you're calm. Just go with them. I'll have a lawyer come and represent you, and we'll have you back out on the street in no time. Then we'll go and talk to some people about your uncle.'

'I'm not going to the cop shop,' I say. I take the pill but don't swallow it. It's resting on the back of my tongue, a trick I perfected in prison when they kept fucking around with my meds. 'When they get me in there, I don't come out. And I can't stay here either. Someone tried to have me bumped off last night, and if they find out I'm here, they'll come for a second try. They shot Rab's dog. I got to find them and kill them a whole bunch of times.'

'Please, just—'

I stop her talking with my lips. I press them on hers hard and fast, and she pulls back for just a wee second before she's kissing me too. She makes a grunting noise, and her breathing speeds up, and then she's shoving her tongue down my throat. And I'm thinking, fuck yeah. I have to swallow the pill to get it out of the way, but I don't mind this time. I reach my hands round behind her and feel her arse, and then she presses closer up against me. She grunts a little more. Then I whisper the name Jenny, and she steps back.

'No, Mack, we've talked about this.'

'I know; I'm sorry.' I pull her in again and give her a playful kiss, just a short one to win her back around. 'Beth, I need to get away. Then later on, once I've got my shit done, we can go somewhere nice and start this again. In a naked way.'

She looks at me. There's uncertainty in her eyes, but something else too. She's up for it, and she's horny as fuck. Are all psychiatrists this much fun, or did I just get lucky?

'Okay,' she says. 'But call me as soon as you're away.'

'Abso-fucking-lutely.'

'Wait a couple of minutes.' She rubs my nose with her thumb. 'I'll distract them.'

I step up close to the curtain and hear her walking across the tiled floor. She strikes up a conversation, and the voices that come back in reply are Baldy's and Perera's. The conversation gets more heated and moves further away. I stick my head out of the curtain and see Beth giving them a real argument over something. They've turned their backs to me, and Beth's taking a few steps in the other direction, trying to lead them away, but they're pros. They stay exactly where they are. There's not going to be a way out past them.

I look the other way. There's a door at the other end, past all the other cubicles with drawn curtains. That'll be worth a try. Baldy turns his head. He's side on to me now, as he's keeping watch with his periph . . . peripher . . . side vision. I duck back behind the curtain. Baws. Beth isn't going to be able to keep them for long. I need another way out. Like Steve McQueen.

Wait.

I'm being an idiot.

I step back to my bed and then look at the curtain to the side. At the end, by the wall, there's a gap. I push through to the next cubicle. A little old lady looks up at me in surprise from the old lady magazine that she's reading. I put my finger to my lips and smile, give her a little of my charm. I walk around her bed and then through into the next cubicle. Some fat dude is out cold, with a big bandage at the end of his leg, where his foot should be. In the next cubicle over are a doctor and nurse fucking away quietly on the bed. They don't notice me at first because they're deep into it. They both gasp when they see me, but it's at the same low volume that they've been screwing at, so I don't think anyone hears. I hurry past them and through the next curtain. This is the last one on the row, with a wall on the opposite side of the bed. A guy is flat on his back with a mask over his face. He seems to be having difficulty breathing, and the mask is either pumping air in or taking it out—I can't be sure. On a chair beside the bed are his belongings. There's a rather nice leather coat, a brown thing, like in a submarine movie. There's a pair of black jeans too. He doesn't look like he needs either of them. I'm sure if I stop to explain how I need a disguise to evade the *polis*, he'll agree that a German submarine captain is the perfect disguise.

I slip on the jeans. They're a size too big, but there's a belt I can tighten to hold them up. I nod my thanks to the guy as I pick up the coat, and he stares at me with watery eyes. It looks like he really loves my new leather. I slip my arms into it and try it on, and instantly feel like the star of an action film. Well, I always feel like the star of an action film, but I've just promoted myself from Roddy Piper to Kurt Russell.

149

I step out into the room, bold as brass, like Snake Fucking Plissken. I stand and watch the two coppers for a second. Beth sees me and her eyes widen a little, but she keeps it under control, and I get away with it. I blow her a kiss and then turn and walk out through the door behind me.

Thirty-One

Beth was right. The pill has calmed me down, and my head is clearer. I can think straight now.

For instance, I notice that I'm not wearing any shoes.

That's a problem with my disguise, right there. I'm pretty sure German submarine commanders wore shoes. Bruce Willis went barefoot in *Die Hard*, but we haven't reached that stage yet. It would be nice to throw the dog killer off a building, though. I'll make a note of that for later.

I could have taken the shoes from the guy with the missing foot, back on the ward. It would only really have been half a theft since he's only going to need one from now on.

Too soon?

Okay. Time to use this nice clear head and think. Where will I get shoes in a hospital? There's bound to be a lost property room around here, but I can't go asking for it. I turn a corner and find myself in the A&E waiting area. People are slumped in plastic chairs. Some are calm and sleepy, some have bits of metal sticking out of them, a couple are screaming. It looks like a fun crowd. I guess my bare feet aren't going to draw that much attention.

The front entrance is across from the waiting area, on the other side of the seats. Two uniformed cops are standing there, deep in conversation. I don't know for sure that they're here because of me, but it's best to assume.

Two guys stand up in the waiting area, and both have their eyes fixed on me. One is a couple sizes larger than me, with big muscles beneath a tight T-shirt; the other's short and skinnier. I've seen them before somewhere. They'll have been at some party I was at. Bottom line: if they know me, they're here to get me.

I smile at them and offer a comedy wave, then turn around and head back the way I've come. I see the door for the men's room. Perfect. I push on through and then try to put as much distance between the door and me as I can before they follow. The skinny one is the first through, followed a few seconds later by the larger dude.

The big guy leans back on the door, keeping it closed with his weight, and watches as the skinny guy springs towards me off the balls of his feet.

Two of them.

One of me.

I'm down a pint of blood, and I'm barefoot.

In any other situation, they'd beat the shit out of me. But they've picked the wrong place to try it. There's no room in here for them to make the numbers count. I duck my head aside to avoid the skinny guy's leading fist, then throw my weight into the rest of him. I body-check him to the side, and he lands on the sink, the small of his back smacking into the hard edge of the porcelain. The sink cracks and the guy spasms. He yelps, then lands on the floor and throws up. Do I imagine the smell of piss? No. There's a dark stain spreading across his jeans. Nice trick—I'll remember that. The big guy seems stuck for a second. He wasn't expecting this. Sometimes the bigger guys are the worst fighters. They never have to do it. In a quick fight, when it's all about surprise and power, they can do fine. When they have time to plan, to think, they panic.

I jump him before he can decide what to do. I hit him in the forehead, slamming his head back into the door. Then I follow with a hard knee to his baws. I'm a classy guy. He kneels forward, and I elbow him in the side of his face as he goes down. Just for effect.

'Who sent you?'

He looks up at me, then shrugs and spits at my feet. I kick him in the face, and his nose breaks. Blood spurts over my toes. Great. I turn back to the other guy.

'Listen, Piss Stain, this is the second time today I've got up close and personal in the lav. The last guy ended up with me putting a knife to his family jewels, so let's just say that so far you're coming out ahead.'

He thinks about this and stays silent. It looks like he's buying it. That's good, because I don't have a plan B.

'So all I want,' I say, 'is a name. And just one more thing. Shoes. I want your shoes. Unless you've pissed all over those too.'

Back out in the reception area a couple of minutes later, I hear some shouting. I can see Baldy and Perera over the other side, having a hurried conversation with the uniformed coppers, who are now heading into the ward where they'd been keeping me. I pull the collar of the coat up a little higher and walk out through the seated area and to the front door. These new shoes squeak on the floor. I don't like them. I'll steal a better pair later.

Outside I remember we're in the middle of a heatwave. The afternoon sun is burning down on me and my new coat, and the sweat starts straight away. I keep it tight around me, though. I want to be well away from here before I open it up. There's a taxi rank by the door. I climb into the first one.

The driver asks me where I want to go.

I smile.

Piss Stain gave me the name. I know who ordered them to kill me. It has to be the same person who ordered the hit last night. The same fucker who killed Rab's dog. I don't know why yet, but there'll be plenty of time for that.

Gilbert.

I'm coming for you.

There are plenty of ways for you to die.

Thirty-Two
Jim

Sam.

I need to warn Sam.

She's in over her head. I know she's only trying to impress me. She thinks what I want is for her to keep the business going, like I can't see through her lies every time she tells me things are going well.

Why the hell would I want her to be in this game? I've seen what it does to families, to people, to me. It's my fault; I talked it all up, made her think I loved the job.

Got to get to the phone.

Got to concentrate.

Find a thing in my head and cling to it. Sam. Phone Sam. Help Sam.

I climb out of my chair and wobble on my feet. Annoying. I used to remember how to walk. Now I need a stick or a frame to help. The memory is in here somewhere—just need to find it. One leg, two legs; there—got it.

What am I doing, again?

Got to concentrate.

Think of Sam.

She needs her dinner cooked. No. Wait. That's an old memory. Push it away. Focus, Jim, just this fucking once. You can do this, you stupid old man. Stay here. Stay now. Stay with it.

The job.

She needs to quit.

Keep moving. Keep thinking. Keep remembering.

She doesn't know about the deal I made. She'll never look at me the same way again if I tell her. I'll die if I never see her smile again. No. Move. Need to do it. It's time.

Andy can't be trusted. Gilbert and Neda—they're dangerous. They'll break the deal. They promised to leave Sam alone, but if she goes messing . . .

I get to the phone. What's her number? What's her fucking number? Where do I keep it? Is it next to where I put the memory of Sam winning that race on sports day when she was nine? No, why would I keep it there. Maybe—wait! It might be next to the last time I talked to her mum; that was on the phone, right? Keep the number next to the phone. I try and think, but it's not there. It's never been there.

I never got to see her face that last time. She sounded so distant. So far away.

Who am I thinking of?

Back to Sam. Her number. Need her number. She's late home from school, and I'm worried. I need to call her. I always needed a notebook to remember numbers. Where is my notebook? It's on my desk, in my office.

Where is my office?

Why am I stood by the phone?

Sam. That's it.

She's in trouble. She's going to phone me.

'Jim? You wanting to call someone, Jim?' The nurse puts a hand on my shoulder, looks into my eyes.

156

Hope my mum doesn't see me talking to a pretty lady. She'll be home in a minute, and my bedroom is a mess.

'Come with me,' the nurse says. 'We'll get you settled back down.'

PART FOUR

'It doesn't matter the who or the why. All that matters is the dead.'

—*Neda*

Thirty-Three
Sam

They drove me in a taxi, of all things. The old guy sat in the front, tapping his fingers on the steering wheel to some oldies station playing very polished folk music. The dinner lady sat in the back with me, pressed in close.

We took the M8 motorway, the winding strip of concrete that circles the city like some Victorian torture rack, and dodged between the rush-hour cars. We pulled off at the Govan exit, turned in the other direction, along Bellahouston Park. We came to Dalkeith Avenue, a tree-lined, middle-class road with large houses and gated properties. The taxi eased onto the driveway of a freestanding red-brick house, and someone stepped out from behind us to shut a metal gate across the driveway.

Old Guy and Dinner Lady led me silently to the front door. I wondered, was I supposed to tip them for the taxi ride? The hallway was large, with a tiled floor and wooden staircase, dark green paint above the wainscoting. I was pointed into the first door on the left, which led into a living room that had the same theme as the hallway, but with deep red instead of green. Three leather sofas were arranged around an open fireplace, and there were shelves lined with old leather books either side of the bay window. The sort of books people pose with rather than read.

I lowered myself into one of the sofas and instantly felt like I'd been sitting there my whole life, a comfortable life lined with sleep and relaxation. Dinner Lady asked if I wanted a drink, and I asked for a milky coffee. She was very soft-spoken and friendly, nothing like the person who had almost broken my arms earlier that day. A small dog walked in. I didn't know the breed, but it was furry and bouncy and looked like a puppy that was doing an impression of a cat. It sniffed around my feet and then pressed up in between my legs, presenting its head for a fuss. I rubbed the top of his head and then his floppy ears.

An elderly man stepped into the room and called out the name Bobby, and the dog ran out of the room. 'Sorry to summon you out with such short notice,' he said, 'but my days are pretty full at the moment.'

He took a seat opposite and smiled gently at me. He looked like Richard Branson, give or take twenty pounds, and spoke with a soft English accent, so I instantly wanted to distrust him.

'Your father is Jim Ireland, right?'

I nodded.

'Ah, and you're that wee girl of his, the one who wanted to be an artist?'

'Do I know you?'

'You wouldn't remember. I came to your father's house a few times. He was showing people your photographs, talking about art college. Looks like you changed your mind, though, eh?'

'And your name?'

He stood back up and took my hand again. 'Oh god, I'm sorry. It's just been a while since I walked into a room and had to introduce myself. I'm Ryan Hillcoat.'

'Sam Ireland.'

'Pleasure. And may I say, you grew up well, my dear. I can see your father in you too.'

He talked like an old head teacher of mine, a gentle professor pose I was trying hard not to be distracted by. Any man who had me invited over at the end of a gun was not someone I wanted to start chatting with.

'Mr Hillcoat, did you call me here to talk about old times?'

'You're direct like him too. I like that. No, I have a wee bit of a problem. And it seems you're mixed up in it. Tell me, please, who hired you to make that delivery to Mr Anderson?'

When he said 'Mr Anderson', I wanted to say 'Neo'.

Not sure he'd get the reference, though.

'That was a private business matter.'

'You like discretion. I saw it shine through in the news item—the insurance case? Yes, you seem to know how to handle things the right way. If we might try this another way, I'll make a few assumptions, okay?'

I nodded.

'You were hired by a city solicitor to serve legal papers on Mr Anderson. You don't know what the papers were or on whose behalf the solicitors were acting.'

I sipped my coffee. 'Go on.'

'And you've gathered by now that you're not going to find Mr Anderson alive. I hope you still get paid for your efforts today.'

'Me too.'

He stared at me for a while, but it was a benevolent stare, patient. Again the professor act.

'Miss Ireland—or, sorry, is it Ms? Right, yes. You don't know me, so there's plenty here that you won't know. I want to level with you, but I've learnt the hard way not to trust people in this city. Can I trust you?'

'I'm not sure either of us has a pressing motive to trust the other right now.'

'True enough. Okay. A show of faith, then. I'll start levelling with you on a few things. For instance, I hired your father a long time ago. He worked a case for me that he never managed to solve.'

'What was it?'

'The murder of a young woman—a girl, really—who was working for me. Jenny Towler. Do you remember it?'

I did. There was an era when it was the story that all parents told their daughters to keep them in line. The story about the young woman who went out one night with her high school sweetheart, without anyone else around, and got butchered. My dad had told me about it in those same tones, but he'd never mentioned working the case.

'They caught the guy who did it, right?' I searched my memory for a name, but it wasn't there. 'It was her boyfriend. They'd been to school together; he had some kind of mental problem?'

Hillcoat neither nodded nor shook his head, but gave a shrug that was halfway between the two. More an acknowledgement that what I'd said was one accepted version of events than an endorsement that it was correct.

'Malcolm Mackie. He's a bit of a legend in town off the back of Jenny's death. Here's the thing, though, Sam—I can call you Sam? Here's the thing. Mackie is the nephew of Rab Anderson.' This was the first time he'd said *Rab*, and he failed at it like most Englishmen. Most will cop out and say *Rob*. 'And Jenny—well, she worked for me. She was a sweet young woman.'

'So you wanted to make sure justice was done. But they got the man who did it, so there was nothing there for my dad to solve.'

'The case is far more complicated than you know,' he said.

I heard someone walking down the hallway outside, and Hillcoat stood up and waved through the open door. Another woman stepped into the room. She was shorter than me, with blond hair and curves. She was carrying about ten pounds too much, but between her curves and her broader shoulders, she was getting away with it. She had a nice face, one that I wanted to trust.

'Dr Elizabeth Carter,' Hillcoat said. 'This is Sam Ireland, the private investigator I told you about.'

I stood up to shake her offered hand.

'Call me Beth,' she said. Her accent carried the roll and flick of Newcastle. 'Mackie is innocent. I think he was framed.'

Thirty-Four

'Innocent?'

Beth sat down beside me on the sofa. A little too close, like she didn't understand personal space. Then she said she was a psychiatrist, and I thought, *That figures.*

'I don't think Mackie did it,' she said. 'I've got to know him well over the last few years, since Ryan got me in as Mackie's therapist.'

'I'm not sure any of this is legal,' I said.

'No, and that's why it's important that we can trust you,' Hillcoat said. 'I pulled a few strings to get Dr Carter attached to Mackie's case, and it would ruin our case if news of that got out there.'

'And what is the case—you want to prove Mackie is innocent?'

'I feel responsible for the poor girl's death. Jenny came to work for one of my Glasgow firms,' Hillcoat began. 'She'd some work experience in the office, filing paperwork, answering phones, and everyone seemed to like her, so she was hired on full-time when she left school.' He scratched his nose between sentences, as if doing so was peeling away a layer of memories. 'She was a nice girl. Bright, asked a lot of questions. But that was the problem: she was starting to ask a lot of questions. Wanted to know how we worked, what we were doing, what we were investing in. It was brought to my attention, and I had a word with her, a friendly warning, if you like.'

'Warning?'

'Bad word. More like advice. You see, I get a lot of people prying into my business. There are a lot of people who stand to gain by finding out my plans. I'm used to having to warn them off before they cause trouble. We all liked Jenny, and so I told her she had a big future with us, but that she was going to need to pick her friends carefully if she was going to stay with us.' He scratched his nose again. I spotted it for what it was: a sign of guilt. 'A few days later she was dead.'

'Mackie has always had troubles.' Beth took up the story. Still too close to me. 'All of his evaluations from a very young age talked about him having flights of fantasy and paranoia. Later on he was diagnosed with schizophrenia, and he wasn't treated properly back then. But there's nothing to suggest he was violent.'

'Aside from the dead young girl.'

She gave a patient smile and let that go for a second before starting again.

'There's nothing before that incident to show any kind of anger or violence in Mackie. It's only since then, since he saw her body and then served time in prison, that he's begun to exhibit a temper. And a pretty extreme one at that. But it goes away when he's on beta blockers. He calms down, and his pre-existing mental illness becomes perfectly manageable again.'

'So you think it was Jenny's death that triggered the anger, rather than his mental illness? Couldn't it be the other way round, and the murder was just the first episode, his illness getting out of control?'

'Sure.' She nodded. 'That's one way to see it, and that's what they said in the court case. His doctors at the time were all assuming he was guilty, so nobody contested that view. But I think it's the other way round. I think someone used his illness as an excuse, as a way to set him up. I've seen the love letters he wrote to Jenny. He still writes them. I think the anger we see in him now is post-traumatic.'

'You think it's grief?'

If I took what she was saying at face value, it had a certain logic. If someone else had killed Jenny Towler, it would be a convenient way out to frame Mackie. Nobody would ever think twice about his guilt. Nobody ever does. The press are always running scare stories about psych patients with knives or guns, and it would have been even worse back then.

But that was only if I chose to take them at their word. And there were too many leaps of logic. There was no reason to follow their breadcrumbs into this maze. Above all of that, I was feeling an anger. A young woman had died, been murdered, and we were discussing the case as if it was all about Hillcoat and Mackie.

'I still don't see it,' I said. 'The easiest and simplest explanation is still that Mackie killed her, and he went down for it. Why would anybody want to kill Jenny over your business affairs? Why is it all about you, and where does my father come into it?'

'All fair questions.' Hillcoat stood up and stepped over to the doorway. 'Follow me.'

He led us upstairs. I wasn't feeling comfortable. I was alone with two people I didn't know, locked inside a large house, and they were talking about murder. If he hadn't made a point of mentioning my father, I'd have found a way out straight away. But I couldn't help myself. I needed to know.

On the next floor up, which was decorated in much the same theme as downstairs, except with a much deeper carpet, he opened the door onto a small room that had been turned into an office. There were maps across the walls, with pins in them covering half of Glasgow, and the large desk that took up most of one wall was piled with papers. I stepped into the office with him, and Beth stayed out on the landing. I pretended not to notice that she was blocking the door. Hillcoat pointed at the nearest map, which was a close-up of the East End. The development areas for the Commonwealth Games had been circled, and photographs had been stuck around the map, showing the various new buildings.

I looked at the pictures and then back at Hillcoat.

'You're a developer?'

'I'm an artist.' He laughed. 'Sorry, I know that sounds pompous. But there is an art to it. I'm more of an investor than a developer. An empty field a hundred yards from anywhere might be worthless for twenty years, but once someone wants to run a motorway across that field, or build a sports arena or a hospital, then it becomes a gold mine. And that's where the art comes in, knowing the right place and the right time.'

'So all these sites, they're yours?'

'Not all, but quite a few. There's a lot of money flowing into Glasgow at the moment, if you know where to look. Some places in the UK will never be valuable, and some will never stop being valuable. But Glasgow's one of the areas that comes in and out of fashion. Every generation or so, it has a period when people want to invest, and I manage to be here when it happens.'

'It can't be guesswork. If the money's coming in through community development grants or through something like the Commonwealth Games, then there are people making the decisions on where to invest. All you need to do is know the right people.'

He smiled at me and gave me a look like an old teacher who was pleased with his student. 'Yes, and I always know the right people.'

'So you think this is what got Jenny Towler killed? Someone tried to use her to get information on where to invest or where the next big deal was going to be, and they got mad when she didn't deliver?'

'Some version of that story, yes.'

'Okay. Maybe you're right, maybe you're wrong; but what does it have to do with me being hired to find Rab Anderson? Just because he's Mackie's uncle, that doesn't have to tie any of this to what I've been doing today.'

'Someone tried to kill Mackie last night.' Beth stepped into the room to join us. 'Two men with guns. They shot him in the leg, and he almost bled to death. I just got back from visiting him in hospital. And someone shot Rab's dog too. I found the body this morning.'

'This would have to be an epic level of coincidence, don't you agree?' Hillcoat turned towards me again. 'Anderson goes missing on the same night that someone tries to kill his nephew. Do we really think the universe has that good a sense of humour? Find out who took a pop at Mackie, and you'll find out who killed Rab. Along the way, I think we'll find who killed Jenny Towler.'

I already had a name. Gilbert Neil. All the signs were that he was behind it. But Neda had mentioned that it went higher, that there were names she didn't want to give. I had that warning ringing in my ears, and I was going to save Gilbert Neil's name until I'd covered other angles. I still didn't really trust any of these people. Having the name gave me power, and giving it away might set me up for a fall.

'Okay,' I said. 'But how does my father figure into all of this?'

'I hired Jim to find the real killer. He believed my story, believed it enough, anyway. He spent a couple of weeks looking into it while Mackie's trial was grabbing all the attention, but then he simply quit one day. He said there was nothing to find and that we should all let it go.'

'My dad was good at his job. If he said there was nothing to find, then there really was nothing to find.'

'Your father only ever told me one lie,' he said. 'Something scared him off the case. What I'm wondering, Sam, is just how badly you want to find out what it was your father knew.'

Thirty-Five

The taxi driver was called Murdo. He was waiting out in the car with the dinner lady. Her name was Senga. You have to love Glasgow; once everyone figured we had enough people named Agnes, they just reversed the letters and started again.

Hillcoat gave me an envelope full of cash and told me to call it a retainer. I didn't bother counting it. I'd do that when I got home, and laugh and jump around a little.

Murdo and Senga had been my first leads of the day, the first people to warn me off looking for Rab. I didn't trust them, and I hesitated as I walked over to them. I didn't want to get back in the car.

That's when Murdo gave me their names.

'I wouldn't trust me either,' he said with a smoker's cackle. 'But Senga's got a heart of gold. Wouldn't hurt a fly.'

'I remember.'

'Sorry about earlier, hen,' Senga said. 'We're used to warning people off, protecting Rab. People come in looking for him all the time. Want money, or a fight, or just to say they met him.'

'That's why you told me he was in London?'

'Aye, that's our usual line.' Murdo pulled my purse from his pocket and held it out for me. 'I think someone was counting on that. Using us. Whoever done for Rab knows us too, and how we work. Knew we would play dumb if people came looking for him. Gave them time to cover their tracks.'

I took the purse and stepped past him, climbing into the back of the taxi. They both slid into the front, and I waited until the engine was turning over before asking my next question.

'Any ideas who did it?'

Murdo looked at me in the rear-view. 'All I know is who's talked to me about Rab in the last couple of days. There have been a lot of questions—yesterday and today. One of them has done it.'

'Can you give me the list?' I still bit back on the one name I had. 'That'll be my starting point.'

Both Murdo and Senga watched me silently in the mirror for a while. It was still light outside, but the temperature had dropped. That odd Glasgow summer chill was in the air, where you need a jacket but can still die of sunstroke if you fall asleep in the park.

'When you find out who it is,' Murdo said, 'how's about you let me know first, before you tell the old man. Give me a run at the guy. Give me a chance to make things right my own way.'

'You and Rab go back?'

'Aye. All our lives. Grew up together.'

'So how come you're working with Hillcoat now? I don't get the impression that he and Rab have ever been on the same side—not with the Mackie situation.'

'You ask the right questions.' He pulled off the motorway by Shawfield, the greyhound racing track that my dad had taken me to a few times when I was younger. 'The thing with Mackie was strange. Rab was never the same after that. I think it affected him— he didn't want to be involved in all the same old stuff after he saw

175

what happened to his nephew. That's when he started trying to ease out of it, write the books and move on.'

'And you working with Hillcoat?'

We paused at traffic lights. He used this as an excuse to stay quiet for a moment, pretending to concentrate on the lights as they changed.

'Rab changed and so did I. I'm getting old. I don't want to be keeping up with the kids any more. I'd rather sit and drink and read the paper. Keep an eye on my family and friends. When they grabbed Rab, they changed the rules. Me and Hillcoat both want them stopped.'

We pulled up outside my flat but stayed in the car. I wanted to ask more questions, but I wasn't going to invite them in. They'd already been in, sure, but that wasn't by my choice.

'When was the last time you saw Rab?'

'Last night. He was drinking at the Pit, him and Mackie. They were both steamboats, absolutely gone. Mackie was upset, crying over something, and Rab talked him into going to the brothel on Copland Road.'

'What was he upset about?'

'His psychiatrist had been getting into his head, making him talk about the murder over and over until he was convinced he hadn't done it. He was asking Rab to help him figure out who set him up.'

Rab finds out Mackie wants to investigate the murder.

Rab talks Mackie into going to the brothel.

Mackie gets shot at the brothel.

The maths didn't look good for Rab, and I couldn't be the only one thinking it, but I decided now wasn't the best time to say that out loud. I kept it on-topic.

'Was Rab fine when he left the Pit?'

'Aye. A bit emotional after having to deal with Mackie, but that's just what the drink does to you. He made a couple of phone calls—one I know was to Gary Fraser—then he got up and left.'

'Gary Fraser?'

'Aye. You'd find him at Lebowskis. He's a dealer, maybe can get a few guns from time to time. Useful guy to know, but I don't know what Rab wanted from him because Rab never deals with guns or drugs.'

I asked again for a list of the people who'd spoken to Murdo about Rab in the last two days. I stressed I wanted it to be everyone, and he was good to his word. The list he scribbled on a taxi receipt included me and Andy Lambert, from our run-in at the Pit. At least there were two names I could cross off straight away.

Thirty-Six

I watched through the small pane of glass in the front door as the taxi pulled away, and waited until it was out of sight and the sound had faded from the end of the street before turning the lock and putting the chain on the door.

I went from room to room, checking the windows, and found they were all secure. Something that would usually make me feel safe only worked to make me feel worse. They'd got in without breaking anything. They must have got in through the front door without a key.

How?

The flat felt very open and exposed.

I pulled a chair up against the front door, jamming it below the handle. It wasn't much. It wasn't anything, really. It was going to have to be enough to get me through the night. Last night my biggest problems had been paying the rent and trying to run a little faster. Now I was mixed up in an epic-old grudge match that felt like a greater threat with every passing minute.

Best form of defence is to attack. That's what my dad told me once, when he took me to a game at Parkhead, trying to get me into football. Go on the attack, and they can't score. One day involved in this, and I was already reaching for a sporting metaphor. Still, it held. Get it done. Get them out of the way.

My dad's files were in the spare room, the makeshift office. Boxes piled on top of one another, with letters and dates written on the sides. His filing had been sharp and perfect. His cases were broken down by year, and then, within each year, were organised alphabetically by the name of his client. He had a pile of notebooks, ledgers where he kept an index of them, so that every case he'd ever worked could be found with a few turns of the page. When I was going through university, I'd taken over the maintenance of his filing for some part-time work, and one of the first signs that his mind was giving up on him had been when I noticed things being filed the wrong way. I'd sat on it at first, fixing his messes, but it had got worse, and I'd been the one to force him to go to the doctor.

There hadn't been a day since then that hadn't felt like a small betrayal.

I searched the ledger books and found an entry for Hillcoat, then traced the case to the right box, but there was no file for the case. I went back to the books and searched for entries under other names, like Anderson, but there was nothing. I googled news stories from Mackie's court case and confirmed his real name, then checked that in the ledger too. Still nothing.

I called Phil. When he answered, I could hear the sounds of professional wrestling in the background, the shouting and smacking of large heaps of meat onto canvas. He sounded far more awake than the last time I'd called him. At this time of night, he was just starting to come into his own.

'Hey, chum.' He was going to keep this Batman thing going all night. 'What's up?'

'You ever gone through Dad's file boxes?'

'Hell no. You know I made a mess any time I tried to sort it. That's your area.'

'You didn't see us drop anything when we moved them all from the office, did you? There's a file I need, and it's not in the right place.'

'Have you looked through the other boxes? You know he started to get a little cuckoo with the whole system. Maybe he's filed it under the first name or something. Why'd you need it—a new case?'

'No, same one.'

'Sam, I thought we were dropping this.'

'I'll explain later. It's about Dad.'

I hung up and started going through the other boxes, through Dad's entire career, file by file, looking for one in the wrong place. Was Phil right? Had this been an early example of Dad's mind going? I felt guilty, but part of me wanted that to be the case. I didn't want to think that he'd deliberately lost the file. Why would he do that? There was no answer that led anywhere good.

The old answer machine was flashing. I clicked on the button, and the message played. It was from Fiona Hunter, and she didn't sound happy.

'Ms Ireland, I think we need to have a meeting. We had a visit today from a police officer, a Detective Inspector Andrew Lambert, and he seemed to have knowledge of your assignment that could only have come from you or from the file we gave you to deliver. I will welcome your views on this at 9.15 tomorrow morning, in my office.'

Great. At least I knew the exact moment that my chances with that company were going to be shot down in flames.

Wait—hang on. Andy? How did he know who I was working for? And why would he visit them? I looked again at the list Murdo had given me. Andy's name was on there, before mine. I'd assumed it was only there because he'd gone into the Pit for my belongings.

It couldn't be any other reason.

And then there was that wound on his hand, the morning after Rab's dog was killed.

He couldn't be involved.

Could he?

Thirty-Seven

I decided to check out the first lead Murdo had given me. Gary Fraser. I sent Phil a text to meet me outside Lebowskis and caught the train from Bridgeton to the Exhibition Centre station, which was only a few minutes from the bar.

It was not too far to have walked, but I avoided being in the city alone after dark. Glasgow, for all its bravado, was a city that couldn't handle its drink. It got loud, angry and sloppy. Men, women and crazed hen parties trotting up and down the streets, falling over and throwing up. The second reason was rape. There was a culture of it in the city. A woman was getting assaulted or raped every month in Glasgow, and the press barely touched it. Didn't matter where, didn't matter how exposed or public the location—nobody helped. When the Occupy movement were camped out in George Square, a woman was raped in one of the tents. Other campers would later tell the police and press of the sounds, of hearing the woman in distress and crying. Nobody seemed to take the extra step of going to see if there was anything they could do to stop those sounds.

City life always had ways of showing how little it cared about you. If you were a woman, Glasgow had a few extra.

I stepped off the train into the cool evening air. The temperature had dropped even further, and it felt like we might finally get some rain. Honest-to-goodness Scottish weather for the first time in a month. I looked forward to it. I looked forward to moaning about it. I headed up Minerva Street, which was pretty much just car parks and bad driving, and turned onto Argyle Street. Phil was already parked up ahead, on the side of the road I was walking down, leaning against the side of the car and waiting for me.

'What's the rumpus?' he asked.

'What?'

'From a film—never mind. What's going on—we still on the Anderson case?'

'Long story short, we've been hired by someone else to look into the same case. Sort of. It might tie into an old murder, and we're being asked to keep working on it, try and follow the lead back.'

'Murder? Sam? We don't do murders. We do insurance fraud, cheating husbands, background checks on defendants. Police do the murders.'

'They might have got this one wrong.'

I saw him think it through. Whether to keep challenging me or roll with it. It was a look I'd seen in him his whole life; he'd picked it up from our father. Our father who, in turn, had picked it up from looking in the mirror a few too many times.

'Okay,' Phil said, rolling with it. 'So what's the deal here? Who we talking to in Lebowskis?'

'I'm talking to Gary Fraser. You're standing behind me at the bar, looking scary.'

'Gary?'

'You know him?'

'Aye.' He answered as if it should have been obvious. 'I buy weed off him sometimes.'

Well, that changed things. Hard for Phil to play my heavy in the background if he was known in there. Nobody who knew Phil was scared of him. His imposing appearance lasted until precisely ten seconds after he opened his mouth and started talking about eighties cartoons and superhero movies.

A new plan was needed.

'Okay, time for you to play detective,' I said. 'I'll play the heavy in the background, to probably mixed results. You try and get information from Gary.'

'What do we need to know?'

'Why did Rab talk to him yesterday? Does he know where he was going? And is there anything else we can use for information? But don't just come out and ask that, because people get defensive. You need to sneak up on it; talk about anything other than what we want to know, then find ways to sneak the questions in.'

'Gotcha.'

We crossed the road, dodging between the evening traffic because we were too lazy to walk the twenty yards down to the pedestrian crossing. There was no bouncer on the door at the bar, which was unusual for this time of night. Maybe it was a place that never encountered any trouble. Sometimes that was more worrying than a bar that had a small army of bouncers.

It was dark inside, but not in a scary or intimidating way. The lights looked like they had been specifically designed for the exact right pitch for drinkers. Dark enough to protect the fledgling hangovers and put people at ease, but bright enough to remind everyone not to fall asleep. There weren't many drinkers inside, and Phil headed straight for a wiry man seated at the bar. I hung back a few steps, trying to look cool and mysterious, but the man at the bar only had eyes for me as we walked over.

'Phil, how you doing?' The man extended a hand to shake Phil's. 'Who's your bodyguard?'

'Gary, this is Sam, my sister. Sam, Gary Fraser.'

He looked at ease, totally at home. His stubble was carefully sculpted, and his hair combed to look uncombed. He looked like he practised being at ease, but it suited him. I leant in and shook his hand. I waited for his eyes to move up to meet mine before I spoke.

'How you doing, Gary?'

'I'm great,' he said. 'So are you.'

Groan. I felt my cheeks flush, but it was anger rather than embarrassment. In moments like this I lost all sense of my own safety and security, and went for being as annoying as I could. Phil had already started some ambling introduction, small gossip about other dealers, but I took hold of the conversation.

'So, Gary, why did Rab Anderson come to see you last night?'

His eyes popped wide, like a cartoon, before he regained the cool indifference that he'd clearly spent years practising. He looked from me to Phil, then back to me. He noticed my face for sure now. I'd forced him to take me seriously.

'Direct, aren't you?' he said. 'Anderson came here, but it's personal business.'

'He's dead. He doesn't have any personal business any more.'

'Dead?' His face cracked into real emotion again—this time it was surprise. 'Are you sure?'

'Neda Tenac told me.' I decided to lean on the name, try and let him imagine I was more connected than I was. 'And people are talking, saying he came to you last night for a favour.'

He thought about this. Phil stayed silent, but I could see him looking around the bar, casting glances at the other drinkers, watching for any movement. Gary set his drink down on the bar and ran his tongue along his teeth inside his closed mouth.

'Who's been talking?'

'Pretty much everyone I've spoken to. They're all wondering what he came to you for.'

'Nobody knows?'

'Doesn't seem so.'

Gary checked his watch and then turned back to Phil for the first time since the introductions. 'You got your car?'

Phil nodded.

'Let's go.'

He stood up off his stool and reached behind where he'd been sitting to lift up a canvas bag. He nodded for us to get moving, and we let him lead the way. We headed outside, where I felt a little rain, finally. We crossed the road, with Phil pointing Gary towards the car. Gary climbed into the back seat and slid down, keeping as low as he could, and Phil and I sat in the front.

'Where we going?' Phil asked, the key in his hand hovering a few inches from the ignition.

'Nowhere,' said Gary. 'We wait here.'

'For what?' I turned round to see him, but he waved me back.

'Stay facing forward,' he said. 'We don't want anyone to notice us. Just look like you're sitting in your car chatting to your man there.'

'What's going on?' Phil made eye contact with Gary in the rear-view. 'Why the sudden panic?'

'Rab came to me last night, asking for money. Sixty grand. I agreed to have it for him today, a loan.' In the mirror I saw his hand pat the bag on the seat beside him. 'I've had it with me all day. Been a pain in the arse going to the toilet with my bag; makes me look like I'm shooting up.'

'Well, Rab's not going to be coming back for it,' I said.

He stared at me in the mirror. 'With all the blether about him going missing, I got worried. Been sitting here all day with the cash, and all it took was someone working out what I'd agreed with him, and they might come and hassle me. I figured if he wasn't going to be coming for it, I'd take it home.'

'Right.'

'So I left him a few voicemails, sent him a few texts—just innocent ones, asking what time he wanted to meet, if the deal was still on—nothing detailed.'

'Okay.'

'He texted me back half an hour ago. Said he was lying low, and that he'd come pick up the money around 8.30.'

I looked at the clock on the dash. It was 8.30 on the dot.

'So if Rab's dead'—Phil asked the obvious—'who texted you? Who's coming for the money?'

We sat in silence. Rain started to spatter on the window and drum on the roof. Light at first, then picking up, turning into one of those soft summer rains that set the air free. We watched people walk along the street. We watched traffic speed by.

We watched Andy Lambert walk up to Lebowskis and step inside.

Thirty-Eight
Lambert

Pregnant?'

Lambert paused. How the hell to respond? Certain moments came along as tests, he'd always thought, and you were defined by how you reacted to them. He'd never wanted children. They'd always been clear on that, and Jess had agreed.

No kids.

No drama.

No hassle.

Two adults getting to live their lives free of any ties or links. Never needing to worry about whether they could have the holiday they wanted because the hotel might not allow children. Never having to worry about saving up for university fees in case the government reintroduced them. And deep down for Lambert, he knew, never having to stop and think about occasionally screwing someone else while the mother of his children was at home waiting to see his smile.

And yet, neither of them had ever discussed him having the snip. Surely a conversation that would have come up at some point if they were both locked in to the idea.

The ground stopped spinning beneath his feet.

This was one of those moments. He was about to be defined.

'Are you sure?' he asked.

'Yes. Two different test kits. I've been feeling a little crampy the last few days, and my period would have been due around the end of last week. I've been really tired, but then there's nothing new in that.'

'You always feel tired during term time.'

'Yeah, so I ignored it at first. But then my boobs got really sore, and I looked up all the symptoms online, then bought two different test kits. It's happening. I'm cooking.'

She looked at Lambert, and he could see in her eyes that she was waiting to read him, to see what he wanted to do.

'Well, I . . . uh, I mean.' He stopped and tried again. 'That is, ummm . . .'

Jess smiled and squeezed his hand.

'Apparently pregnancy turns men into gibbering wrecks,' Lambert said.

They both laughed, and a little of the tension eased from the room.

He realised the one thing he needed to ask. 'What do you want to do?'

She rubbed her belly gently, touching it as if there would be something there at this early stage to feel the touch. She nodded, more to herself than Lambert, and smiled.

'I want to keep it,' she said. 'I know we're both old for this, but it feels right—I think?'

Lambert looked at his wife. He turned and stared at the photographs on the wall, their wedding day, fifteen years and a million decisions ago. He thought of how happy she'd been and of the deals he'd had to make with Joe McLean. Lambert had got a promotion and a cushy job, and over the years that was what he'd started to remember most. But that wasn't what had come first.

First had been a young woman with a great smile, a university student training to be a teacher. The world stopped moving beneath his feet for the first time that day.

'Okay,' he said. 'Let's do this.'

Jess leant in and kissed him on the cheek before giving him a warm hug that lasted for five minutes. 'What are we going to do about Dad?' she asked.

'What?'

She pulled away and gave him a look. A 'no shit, Sherlock' look. 'Now's not the time to treat me like an idiot. I'm his daughter. Mum knew it, and I knew it. Even as a child, we had better living conditions than the other cop families. The same kind of living conditions the two of us have had as adults.' Lambert didn't make a move to deny it, so she carried on. 'You turn a blind eye when it's your family. And because you're getting the benefit of it. But it doesn't mean you don't notice it.'

'Okay.'

'But you're not handling it the way he does. I talk to other families. I know you're always in trouble at work. I know you've got a disciplinary coming up and that you've been visiting the therapist for stress. The man I fell in love with, the man I married, was not a man who does dirty favours for Joe McLean.' Lambert started to protest, but she waved the words away. 'Look, I know, okay? I'm not judging. You've been doing what you thought was right, standing by the family.'

'What's changed?'

She rubbed her belly again. 'This is the family now. You, me and the potato.'

'That's your first choice of name?'

'I'm willing to be debated down on that one, maybe to "Spud" or "Chip". I draw the line at "Freedom Fry".'

'I fucking love you, Jess.'

'Don't say it like it's a surprise.' She let a dark smile sit on her lips for a while before slapping him to show it was a joke.

Lambert felt light. There had been weights pressing down on his shoulders for so long, he'd stopped noticing they were there. But once his father-in-law found out about the baby, it would become just one more thing for him to hold over them. Now he'd be emotionally blackmailing two parents about a child's future, rather than a husband about his wife.

'So, what do we do?' he asked. 'About Joe.'

'I've got savings. You've got savings, right? This house is his; neither of us has ever had to make a mortgage payment—how much do we have saved up between us? I've got about forty grand. You?'

Lambert didn't have a figure. He'd been putting three hundred pounds a month into a savings account ever since the wedding, and his defence against dipping into it was to make sure he never saw a statement for the account, never knew how much he had to blow on a stupid car or a trip to Vegas. Plus there was money McLean had given him over the years, kickbacks and silence payments. He'd paid each one into the bank.

He did some quick sums in his head. 'Probably around eighty,' he said.

His phone buzzed and he saw a text from Sam, but ignored it. As far as she knew, he was in bed. It could wait until later. If Jess was fazed by the buzzing of the phone, she didn't show it.

'Okay, so we've got over one hundred grand that we can get to,' she said. 'Who needs my dad? Who needs Glasgow? Is there anything you really treasure that you wouldn't be able to pack into the back of the car?'

Lambert thought about it and, no, all of his belongings were just *stuff*. He hadn't managed to accumulate anything in the last two decades that would break his heart to lose if the house burned down.

'You've got the police pension. We could work out if there's a way to get at that further down the road, and I've got my teacher's pension, the last of the good ones. We don't need to be here. We can just drive somewhere else, start a new life, and work everything else out later.'

'A hundred grand isn't a lot these days. We won't get that far.'

'You kidding me on? A hundred grand is a lot in any year.' She slapped him again, and it was still playful but carried a little more of an edge. 'It'll get us far enough. We'll contact Dad in a year or so, send him pictures of his grandchild.'

Lambert nodded. He said they'd better start packing. Then one of his phones started to ring. It was the unlisted one, and it brought reality back into the conversation. It would be Joe or Gilbert. There was still Rab's dead body in a lock-up in the city, and people who were expecting to see him. He needed to tie up some loose ends before they could run.

Thirty-Nine

The Barge was a well-known local restaurant. It had originally been called The Barge on the Clyde, but the second part of the title had become redundant by its obviousness. The restaurant was a large boat docked on the river, permanently moored beside a refurbished stretch of the riverbank next to a large casino.

It was a restaurant, a bar and a wedding venue. On that particular night, though, it was playing host to a meeting.

Lambert approached the barge from the shadow of the M8, the motorway bridge that crossed the river. The entrance to the restaurant was a metal gangway which linked the dock to the barge, and standing guard on either side of the doorway were two of Neda's people. Two squat men in faded denim jackets, with their collars turned up. Lambert didn't see the guns, but the shapes beneath the denim were easy enough to read. The man on the right of the entrance looked Lambert up and down before nodding for him to enter. The man on the left kept his eyes fixed on the middle distance.

Inside the restaurant the tables had been set for a normal evening's service, but none of the staff was anywhere to be seen. They would be used to this by now, being hustled out and told to come back in an hour, a paid break. Lambert headed through to the large kitchen at the rear. Food was laid out on work surfaces, ready to cook, but there was nobody working on it. Plastic chairs had been arranged in a semicircle, like an AA meeting. In the centre of the circle was a small table that held a pot of coffee and some biscuits.

Lambert was the last to arrive.

Already seated were Gilbert Neil and Joe McLean. Nick, the Polish man who did Gilbert's dirty work, stood in the centre, bending over the table to pour coffee. He looked up as Lambert walked in, but didn't offer a nod. Neda sat at the end of the semicircle, leaning back in the chair, with her beefy arms folded across her chest. She glared at Lambert as he took a seat at the opposite end. She hated cops, and crooked ones were the worst kind. Even though she dealt with them on a daily basis, she never stopped hurling insults their way. Nick slurped at his coffee, then hissed as it burned his lips. He took a seat beside Gilbert.

'Who wants to start?' Neda said, laying on the thickness of her accent for effect. She looked at Joe. 'It was you who called this meeting.'

Joe cleared his throat and leant forward.

'First things first,' he said, looking from Lambert to Gilbert and then finally to Neda. 'We would all like to apologise for the mess at Copland Road. I know you've had to spend money on fixing the problem. We'll pay you back for the costs and losses.'

Neda nodded at the apology. 'Money is—eh.' She made a dismissive gesture. 'I will lose some. But it's the family of Marisha, the woman your hit men killed, who needs to be reimbursed. She was sending money back for her parents. She had a boy; he is without mother now.'

'We didn't send the Venture Brothers,' Gilbert cut in, waving with his hand, like this was the most important point of the evening. 'I don't know who did.'

I think I know, thought Lambert, *but that can wait.*

'It doesn't matter the *who* or the *why*.' Neda's tone was scolding and dismissive in equal measure. 'All that matters is the *dead*. She didn't ask to be shot, and one way or another it's down to you people.'

'You're right.' Joe smiled. 'Aye, that's on us. There's a lot on us in the last couple of days, and we'll put it right. We'll make sure the man responsible for this whole mess is taken out—tonight.'

Lambert saw Joe glance sideways at Nick as he said that, but Nick didn't notice. Then Joe made eye contact with Lambert and nodded. It was a gesture he couldn't miss. A set-up. Nick wasn't to blame for any of this, but he was expendable. He just didn't know it yet.

'A good start,' Neda said. 'I want to see proof. Maybe his balls in a jar. Something to send to Marisha's family as a gift. And then, we come to you fuckers lying to me. You thought you could clean up a mess at my own business without telling me. There is the time and money it has taken to get rid of the police.'

'We'll cover that too,' Joe said. 'And more. Just name the price.'

Neda cocked her head to one side like a child thinking through a puzzle. 'Then maybe you start with some answers. What happened really with Rab?'

'Like you said,' Gilbert cut in. 'It's not the who or the why. All that matters is he's dead.'

'So he *is* dead? You broke our deal. I needed to speak to him first, get information for myself. My business. You've cost me money.'

Everyone in the room turned to look at Lambert, who realised it was his turn to join in the game. He nodded and coughed away the dryness in his throat. 'Had to be done,' he said. 'If he was still alive, we'd all be panicking now.'

Neda shrugged. 'Do I look like I panic? But okay. Rab was trouble. Always. Maybe it was his time.'

Joe stuck his hand out towards her for a shake. 'So we're good?'

Neda took his hand in hers and shook once, holding his eyes with a stare that said, *No, but we're good enough for now.* That's all it ever was in the business. Things were good between people until they weren't; then violence started until it all stopped.

'Okay, the next piece of business, then.' Gilbert nodded to Lambert. 'Who are these people that want a meeting?'

'They're rich; that's all I really know.' Lambert warmed to the subject now they weren't talking about death. 'The law firm who hired Sam Ireland, I visited them earlier, and they have too much money. They hired Sam as a way of smoking out people who worked with Rab, and they seem to know about the business. Or they know enough. They want a slice, and they seem willing to pay.'

Joe laughed. 'They always seem willing to pay. That's how they get you round the table. Then they cut your throats. It's how it's always been done. Hell, it's how I did it when I first wanted in. I just used a police badge to get them to trust me.'

Neda and Gilbert both nodded at that, with distant expressions in their eyes, as if viewing the good old days through a sepia filter.

'All the same,' Lambert said. 'I think it might be worth you meeting them.'

And if they slit your throat, he thought, *then that's one less thing for me and Jess to have to worry about when we blow town. No angry granddad coming looking for us.* Joe stared at Lambert with a neutral expression. Did he know? Had he figured it out?

'Maybe I will,' Joe said after what felt to Lambert like an age.

'I'll arrange it, if you want to meet them. Tonight,' Neda said. 'Security and neutral ground here; you know my price. And if they're as well-to-do as your dirty cop says, maybe we cook for them too.'

Joe nodded.

'Maybe they're for real.' He looked at Lambert again. 'Or maybe they'll be daft enough to try something on. Either way, what can it hurt? Either I get paid, or I get rid of another problem.'

'Speaking of problems,' Gilbert said. 'We still have two.'

'Two?'

'Aye. Mackie slipped my guys at the hospital, beat them up for information. Luckily they were in the right place for treatment. The cops are out looking for Mackie too, but I don't think they'll find him. He's coming for me now, and I'm running out of people willing to go up against him. He's already killed two people and hospitalised two others. I don't fancy waiting around until he announces his presence.'

'And the second problem?'

Before Gilbert could answer, the kitchen doors swung inwards. One of Neda's men from the entrance walked in, followed by Senga. She was carrying a gun, but nobody at the meeting felt threatened.

'Sorry I'm late,' she said. 'But I have a solution to your Mackie problem.'

Everyone filed through to the main restaurant area. A few tables had been pushed aside to clear a space, with a chair placed in the middle. There was a blond woman in the chair, looking scared.

'This is Beth,' Senga said. 'She's Mackie's doctor.'

Forty

Beth looked up at them as they gathered around her. She didn't look hurt, and she wasn't tied down, but Senga had a gun, and guns were very powerful to people who'd never seen one.

She looked familiar to Lambert. He'd seen her around somewhere. Maybe at the police station when she was visiting a patient, or in the witness stand at a court case. Now didn't seem like the right time to ask.

'She and Mackie are sweet on each other,' Senga said. She raised the gun again, making sure the woman got the message. 'She helped him escape your guys at the hospital.'

'How did you get her?' Gilbert said. 'How do you know all this?'

Senga nodded at Joe. 'Ask your man there. He told me to stay with Murdo no matter what, said Andy here was bound to fuck something up and leave a few loose ends and that staying on Murdo would help us see what needed to be done.'

'Aye.' Joe smiled, then cast a hard look at Lambert and Gilbert. 'Both of you. I knew we'd need a backup plan.'

'You were right, Boss. I stuck with Murdo. He's started asking questions now, so he'll need to go. And he's working against us. He went straight to Hillcoat, so he's in it too. Hired Sam Ireland to find out who's killed Rab. He says it's all linked to the thing with Mackie and the Towler girl.'

Lambert stepped closer. This was news to him. What did any of this have to do with Mackie cutting up his high school sweetheart? He was starting to wish he'd skipped the meeting, just gone straight to the lock-up to dispose of Rab's body, the last loose end that traced back to him.

Gilbert waved it away. 'It's not important,' he said. 'What matters is finding out what's going on now, not ten years ago.'

'Well, it does a bit,' Senga said. 'See, he's the one who hired Jim Ireland. Jim never gave up the name, but it was Hillcoat. He knows someone tried to kill Mackie last night, and he's got enough of a head on his shoulders to know that it's all linked in. And Beth here has them all convinced that Mackie's innocent.'

'So hang on. Who killed the Towler girl?' said Lambert. 'How's that all linked in to what we've been doing here? To the business?'

Joe turned on Lambert. 'Keep up or shut up. We've had enough of you already.' He was angry, but it was controlled, focused, all forced out through his eyes.

Lambert took a step back, caught off guard by the anger. He wanted to turn and walk out now, drive home, grab Jess and leave. For all that he'd done, all the lies, the bribes and the violence, he'd always told himself he had rules. Nobody innocent got messed with. Rab hadn't been an innocent. And Mackie, he'd been telling himself, wasn't an innocent either. After all, everyone knew he'd cut up his girlfriend.

But what if he hadn't?

Beth looked at Lambert with a question framed in her eyes. She'd just seen Lambert chewed out by the others, and in that moment, he thought maybe she'd decided they were on the same side. She was looking to him for a way out. Her eyes burned into him until he looked away.

'Shouldn't she be blindfolded or something?' he asked.

'No point,' Gilbert said, before he changed the subject. 'That brings me to our second problem: Sam Ireland.' Lambert and Neda started to object, but Gilbert raised his hands to signal he wasn't finished. 'I know you both like her, and I know we made a deal with her old man, but she's changed the rules. And no matter what you say, Andy, you can't control her.'

Joe nodded.

'We've honoured the deal for a long time,' he said. 'Long enough, I'd say. She's had her chance. Mackie too. This makes everything simple. We kill Sam, we kill Mackie, and we kill Hillcoat. Then the loose ends are tied up, and all we have to worry about are these solicitors that have turned Andy's head.'

Joe shot Lambert another look as he said that last line, daring Lambert to read more into it. Daring him to overthink it. *He knows I'm looking to trick him*, Lambert thought. *Somehow he knows.*

'And my tribute,' Neda reminded them. 'Something to send to Mishka's family. But this is a lot of dead bodies to hide. It's getting messy, Joseph.'

'I have a plan for that—don't worry.'

Joe stepped off to the side and nodded for Lambert to follow. Gilbert moved the other way and motioned for Nick. Lambert got in close to Joe, bracing himself and trying his best to look like he wasn't ready to run.

'Andy, son, sorry I snapped at you. It's just stress is all, and you have been making a mess. A loud mess. You take Nick and get rid of Rab's body. Once he's out of the way, we're into the home stretch.' He paused, watching Gilbert whispering in Nick's ear. Then he looked into Lambert's eyes to make sure he was paying attention. 'Afterwards, we need to do that thing for Neda, give her some blood and a fall guy. Makes sense to do it while getting rid of Rab, two for one.'

Lambert looked over at Nick, being given whatever version of the story was needed for him to walk into a trap. One last bit of violence, one last thing to do, and Lambert could feel like he'd cleaned up his mess.

Neda knelt down in front of Beth and smiled up into her face.

'Hello, hen. You look scared. The guns, eh? Yes, I know. Don't worry about them. Listen, we need your help. Mackie is out there on the warpath, and he's going to cause a lot of damage. To himself too. It's safer if we have a way of controlling him, and you're going to tell us how.'

Beth stared at the gun in Senga's hand and shook her head slowly.

Neda smiled again. 'I know you're trying to be brave, hen. Really, you're doing well. And all these men here? They think they're big and strong. They think they can scare you, and they have guns—guns make them feel like tough guys. But don't worry—they're not going to hurt you.' She leant in closer, eye to eye with Beth. 'It will be me who does that. You can die fast or slow—it's up to you—but you are going to talk eventually.'

Beth started to cry.

'I know, I know,' Neda cooed, like she was talking to a child. 'Would you like a drink first?'

Lambert turned and left. He didn't want to be there.

Forty-One

Lambert drove to the lock-up, with Nick riding shotgun. The conversation on the short drive wasn't sizzling with wit or warmth. Lambert cut occasional sideways glances at his passenger, wondering how the hell he was supposed to take Nick out.

Rab had been tied down, knees broken. Nick had been the one to do the breaking. Lambert had just stepped in at the end to put the full stop on the life story. Nick was not tied down, and nobody had done any breaking of knees or anything else. None that Lambert could see, anyway. Nick was strong and square, like a statue from Easter Island.

'Any ideas how we get rid of Rab?' Lambert said, hiding his nerves. 'I'm new at this.'

'Don't worry about it.'

Nick kept his eyes on the road ahead. Occasionally he flicked his attention to a car coming from the other direction, before settling back on the white lines, watching them as if they might get away.

'You've done this kind of thing before, right? Because I've only ever seen it from the other end. You know, the legal end. My job.'

'Yes.'

Lambert waited for more, but it didn't come. He thought, *Right*, and drove the rest of the way in silence. The space in front of the lock-up was empty, and there was nobody walking past as they climbed out of the car. Lambert took off his jacket and pulled off his T-shirt. It was still just about warm enough to get away with being topless for a few minutes, and it would help with the cleaning up afterwards. He swung the door open and stepped into the darkness.

'We should probably take a look at what state he's in before we decide how best to—'

He shut up when he felt the blade at the back of his neck.

Nick thrust forward to take out Lambert through the back of the neck. The only thing that spared Lambert's life was the halogen lamp. He'd been in the act of bending down to find it in the darkness with his hands, and Nick had chosen that moment to attack, meaning Lambert was already rolling down out of the way.

Lambert didn't get time to think. Nick adjusted to the movement and dropped down after him, letting his full weight bring Lambert down like a sack of potatoes, leading with the sharp blade held in both hands. The knife sliced deep into Lambert's shoulder. All that stopped him screaming was the great weight already pressing down on his lungs. He kicked, then kicked again, connecting with Nick, but not having any effect. Spots of light were bursting in front of his eyes, illuminating the dim space around them. He felt Nick tugging at the knife, trying to pull it out of Lambert's shoulder. That gave Lambert a few inches to move, and he rolled away, over onto his stomach.

Lambert's own weight pressed down on the blade, pushing it deeper. This time he screamed. It filled his head and his thoughts; it filled his vision. A boot caught him in the mouth, shutting him up. Then it came in a second time, connecting with his right eye. Lambert's world went black for a second. Nick was on him again then. Lambert snarled, an animal sound that seemed alien in his throat, and pulled at the knife in his shoulder. It came loose at an angle, slicing a line across his chest as it went. Lambert climbed to his feet as the blade arced out ahead of him in the air, carried by the momentum of his hand pulling it loose.

Lambert felt something as the blade moved, but couldn't be sure if it was contact with Nick. It felt like a knife passing through paper. As Lambert watched, though, Nick took a step back, then another, and then put his hands to his throat. A thick liquid spread over his fingers, and in the darkness it took a few seconds before Lambert realised it was blood. Nick made a gurgling sound. Then he fell inwards on himself, stumbling to the ground in the slow and graceless manner of a drunk. Lambert stood over him as the gurgle faded and the blood spread out across the floor.

Fuck.

Two murders in one day.

Lambert pressed his hand into the shoulder wound while he fumbled for the halogen lamp. When he found it, the neon light filled the room and lit up a scene from a horror film. One dead body lay wrapped in a plastic bundle a few feet away, covered by lime, while another now sprawled at his feet, blood congealing on the tiled floor around them.

It was a set-up.

He was to be Neda's fall guy. Killed in a place where they already knew a body could be hidden away. Then—what? Cut off a body part to offer Neda? He felt light-headed from the wound, and staggered but then righted himself.

What to do now? Run. That was all there was for it. His DNA would be all over this place, but he could maybe cover that by torching it. Maybe. And there was no point going back to the barge—they wanted him dead. *Run.* Go grab Jess and just drive the fuck away. Keep going until the sun came up and they could find the nearest branch of their bank, then drive even further.

He heaved the spare can of petrol from the boot of his car and started pouring it over the two dead bodies and then in each corner of the lock-up. The smell filled his nose, clogging his breathing and making him even more light-headed, but he didn't stop until the can was empty. He pulled a lighter from his pocket and was about to spark up when he caught himself.

Idiot.

Too woozy, not thinking straight.

That's it. Light the flame while you're stood in there. Coated in petrol and breathing the fumes. Why not just finish the job that Nick started. Lambert walked back out to the car and turned around, ready to spark up and throw the lighter in. In the neon glow of the room he caught something else, a small electric light in the corner. He stepped over to it and knelt down. In the bundle of Rab's belongings, searched and dumped last night, was a mobile phone.

Rab's phone.

Lambert thought he'd turned it off. These things were traceable. Lambert had solved a murder once by logging into the victim's email account and activating a function that traced the dead guy's phone. Google Maps had led them straight to the killer, who was still washing the blood off his clothes. It was a schoolboy error, leaving Rab's phone on. Lambert had held the button down until the screen went dark, thought that had done it. Bloody smartphones, you could never tell when you were supposed to swipe the screen and when you were supposed to throw them in the river.

The display said there were a number of texts and voicemails. Rab's phone wasn't password protected, so Lambert could access them. Most were from Gary Fraser. Lambert read a couple, then listened to the most recent voicemail. Gary said he'd been hearing rumours, and if Rab still wanted the package, he needed to call back before 8.00 p.m. Lambert remembered what Gilbert had said earlier, that Anderson was arranging to borrow sixty grand.

That would be a nice going-away present. It would give Lambert and Jess a head start, especially if it took them a while to get at their savings. He texted Gary back to say he'd be there in half an hour.

Forty-Two

Lambert checked himself in the rear-view mirror. He'd wiped away the blood and dressed the wound, using the first aid kit in his car, and then pulled his T-shirt and jacket back on. The fabric stained a little, but it would be manageable for the short time he'd need. By the time more blood soaked through, he'd be back in the car and driving home.

How was he going to get the money from Gaz?

Fuck it. Who cared? He was looking into the eyes of a man who'd killed two people—it wasn't like he needed a plan. He'd parked a couple of blocks over from Lebowskis to give himself a walk up, a chance to see if there was anyone else around who was a threat.

He locked the car and headed down the street, shuffling past people and trying hard not to look like he was favouring his shoulder as he walked. He stepped into the dim lights of the bar and looked for Gary Fraser, but he wasn't there. He asked at the bar, but the barman said Gary had left a couple of minutes before with two friends.

Shit. He'd missed his chance.

A phone started to buzz in his pocket. He had three, so it took him a while to figure out which one it was. Rab's phone was demanding his attention. The caller display said it was Gary Fraser.

He answered the call and put it to his ear, but it wasn't Gary on the other end.

'Turn around,' said Sam. 'I think we need to talk.'

Lambert turned to see Sam in the doorway, with Phil towering behind her.

Forty-Three
Mackie

Bunch of fucking bawbags.

Nobody's telling me where I can find Gilbert. I try the Horse Shoe, but everyone shuts up when I walk in. Not like that scene in a film where everyone turns and stares, with their drinks in their hands. It's just a muting of the volume. The people who don't know me continue talking, drinking and eating. But the guys who know me? Aye, they shut up and stare.

It never seems to be this difficult for Columbo. But then, he always knows who he's after at the start of every episode. Come to think of it, he's of no real use to me as a mentor.

I push Wee Tommy Shittu into the wall beneath his portrait and shout at him, but he says nothing. I stamp Paul Carty's hand into mush, but he stays quiet. Except for the scream. I turn to old Jackie, who used to play snooker with Gilbert in the Imperial on Mitchell Street, but he just throws up over my feet when I hit him in the gut. Then there's Davie Stewart. He tells me I'm asking the wrong questions and that I should look at what's really going on, but then he starts talking about global banking and lizards.

It wouldn't be right to hurt him.

Tam, behind the bar, shouts out that he's called the police and that he mentioned me to them by name. That's just playing dirty. Fine, then—I'll leave. I turn to address the whole room and tell them all that they can suck my boaby. Nobody makes a move. If I had a microphone, I'd drop it and walk out, but I don't, so I just say, 'Boom,' and leave.

I walk round to Neda's shop, but it's all closed up. That's usually no bother—there's always someone in there in case we come calling to do a deal or ask a favour—but this time it's for real. The lights are out, and there's nobody moving in the darkness inside. That's a bad sign.

I have to laugh.

For all Beth's talk of wanting me to have a clear head, I was making more progress when I was all angry and confused. Now I'm just chasing my tail. I have no idea where to find Gilbert and why he'd send those guys to shoot me at—

Wait.

Hang on.

Davie Stewart was right. I don't know how, but he was. I've been asking the wrong questions. My urge to find the fucker who shot Rab's dog has got in the way. I'm assuming it's all the same thing, but Rab pisses people off all the time. Could it all be one big—what's the word?—coincidence?

What I really know is that two guys tried to shoot me. Two guys who knew where I was. I don't know who they were or why they took a shot at me. Gilbert sent the goons to get me at the hospital, but maybe he was just protecting someone. He's not the sort to hire hit men in from outside.

So who the hell were they?

And why did they come for me?

Forty-Four

Back to the beginning.

It's an hour's walk to Copland Road. I could usually do it quicker, but with my bad leg I decide to take it slow. I walk along the Clyde, heading away from the city, past the Barge restaurant and under the motorway, before crossing over at the Squinty Bridge. Then down further along the other side of the river, past the shiny modern science centre and the Imax cinema that looks like a large silver turd, before turning into Summertown Road and then the bottom of Copland Road.

The house is part of Neda's whoring business, and Rab let her use it in exchange for the occasional freebie. He'd sold other South Side houses to her years back, giving her places to set up shop as part of some big peace deal they all negotiated, but he wouldn't give up the house in Copland Road because it had sentimental value. It had been his maw's house.

I see the thick black smoke before I turn the corner at the bottom of the road, and the smell of smoke is in the air. There's the sound of fire engines off in the distance, getting closer, and I can already see the flashing lights of one on the scene. A crowd has gathered in the street, and as I draw near, I see what I already kind of knew.

The Copland house is burning down.

Of course it is. This is Glasgow—things burn down.

Someone is covering his tracks.

I'm one of those tracks, so I don't want to stick around in the crowd in case I get spotted. Whether it's the cops who see me or someone from the other side, either way I'll be fucked. I turn and head back the way I came. I need to slow down and lean on a wall for a few minutes because I'm feeling light-headed and woozy again. I guess this would be why that doctor told me to rest.

Oooops.

I should probably take more of Beth's pills too, and keep this nice clear head of mine, but she's not around and I don't have any on me. I try to find my phone, but I don't have it. When was the last time I saw it? Probably at the whorehouse. And none of these clothes are mine, anyway, so why the fuck am I going through the pockets for my fucking phone? Another problem to fix. I'll add it to the list, right beneath the entry that says 'everything'.

I push off from the wall and head back towards the city, up Govan Road, to the Pit. I guess, really, this is where it all started. This was the last place I spoke to Rab; this was where he sent me away to get my dick wet. It's also the cheapest pint in town, and I can already feel the cool beer on my tongue as I push in through the door.

The room is packed, normal for this time of night. There's nowhere to sit, but when I walk in, someone at the back stands up and clears a stool for me at Murdo's table. Murdo waves for me to join him, and the guy who got up is already heading to the bar to get me a pint. Why would anybody not love a place like this?

I sit down in front of Murdo. I'm not sure how this will go. It's the first time we've spoken since I threatened to chop his boaby off, and as I understand it, people can get a bit arsey about something like that. He just smiles at me, though.

'Good to see you, son,' he says.

Is it?

'Is it?'

'Yeah.' He stretches the word out, showing there's no hard feelings. 'Listen, I owe you an apology. A lot of them, actually.'

'Aye?'

He nods. 'I know a lot more than I did this morning. You were right to be looking for Rab. Someone's grabbed him, and he isn't coming back. I've talked to a few people, to Hillcoat—you know him? Aye, you remember the name anyway. I talked to your doctor, Elizabeth.'

'You talked to Beth?'

My voice went up a wee bit there, like an idiot. He noticed it. I noticed it. We move on.

'Aye,' he says. 'I think she's sweet on you.'

'Yeah, well, I am a stud.'

'Okay.' He smiles, but it's a nervous one. 'She told us she thinks you're innocent, that you were set up over that young lass back in the day—what was her name?'

'Jenny.' My voice cracks again, but this time I don't mind. 'Jenny Towler.'

'That's it. Yeah. So, Elizabeth—Beth—she tells us that she thinks you didn't do it. That someone used you because—well, you know, your issues and that. You were an easy target. And it makes me think about all the times you've said you don't remember doing it and all the times we've talked you into it, saying that you'd blocked it from your memory.' Murdo takes a large pull on his pint.

This bit isn't easy for him. Emotions and all that. 'I always thought we was helping you, aye? Helping you accept it. But now I think maybe we was getting in the way.'

And this jogs memories. Like, *lots* of memories. For a long time, Beth's been trying to get me to talk about the night Jenny died, and lately she's been asking me questions about it. That's where my Columbo things come from—she says watching things like that will help me think the right way. And there's something else, something I can't quite place.

'And then last night,' Murdo carries on, 'last night you was in here asking Rab about it, asking if he could get someone to look into the murder. You were almost out and out saying you thought you'd been set up, and we laughed you off, sent you to the whorehouse to take your mind off it.'

'And that's where all of this happened.' I pat my bad leg.

'Aye, the Venture Brothers. I've heard about that since this morning too. Shit, son, if I'd known it was them that'd gone after you, I wouldn't have been such a dick to you this morning. They're serious business. Someone really wanted you out of the way.'

Well, your dick was certainly involved this morning, I think to myself. I don't say it, though, because he's being all nicey nice, and I don't want to ruin the mood. But am I innocent? Am I really innocent? It wasn't me who killed Jenny? That idea feels right. That idea has always felt right. Why the fuck would I hurt Jenny? I love her. No, *loved* her—get it right, Malcolm. She's dead.

Who killed her?

I'm going to fuck them up.

I feel the emotion bubbling away in my head. Popping sounds come just before the anger. I need to fight this down. I need to keep hold of that light gassy feeling in the pit of my stomach, the one that's about to get my blood boiling. I need to think straight. I need to hold on. Wait—there's another question. Another stupid obvious thing I'm missing.

'Murdo, how much would it cost to hire the Venture Brothers to take me out?'

'Well, for someone like you, someone with a violent streak, it would be probably somewhere about—' His eyes go wide, and his mouth flaps open and closed. He looks at me and then carries on. 'Sixty grand.'

Motherfucker. We both see it. Sixty grand. The same amount Rab was borrowing off Gary Fraser. The same amount he needed to raise in a hurry, not long after sending me round to Copland Road.

'Rab hired them.' I decide stating the obvious is as good a start as any. 'My own fucking uncle wanted me dead. Why?'

I look into Murdo's eyes, but I can tell he's as shocked as I am. He didn't see this one coming. So Beth whispers in my ear, gets me thinking about being innocent. I start talking to Rab, and then he orders a hit on me. He has to be involved. Rab was one of the people who set me up. Rab knew who really killed Jenny T.

I need to find Jenny and tell her.

No, fuck, hold on to it. Jenny is dead.

I need to find Beth and tell her.

I need a pill.

I climb to my feet and head over to the payphone. I dial in one of the few numbers I've ever been able to learn, and wait until Beth's phone starts to ring. It rings for a long time. Long enough that I start to doubt myself, think maybe I dialled the wrong number. I think it back three times, getting the same number each time. No, I dialled right.

Then a man answers.

'Hello?' It's Gilbert. 'Who is this? Is this Mackie? Hello, son. We have a wee present for you here. You might want to hurry up, though. I'm not sure how long she'll last.'

I let go of the feeling in my gut. The anger bubbles and rises. My brain pops away.

I'm coming, Jenny.

This time I'm going to save you.

PART FIVE

'Who died and made you Batman?'

—*Cummings*

Forty-Five
Mackie

We don't go straight round and kill all of the bawbags. We wait. Against my better judgement. Murdo wanted to come along, which was fine—the old guy felt like he had a stake in this, and I respected that. But then he said he wanted Senga to come. She was that dykey one from earlier. Sorry, that's wrong; I'm trying to be good now. She was the unattractive woman from earlier. The one I never mistook for Jenny.

Murdo calls her, and we wait in his taxi.

He bought it years ago as a joke. A black cab that he can drive around. It had come in handy a few times when he'd wanted to slip by the cops and also when he wanted to make a little money on the side. Murdo looks nervous. There was a time when he'd be all about this kind of shite, but he's just a beaten-down old man these days. Probably rather be doing the gardening.

'You got a plan?' he asks.

'Aye. We go round there and kill all of the bawbags.'

'That won't help save your girl.'

'Aye, it will. None of the bawbags will be able to hurt her if they're dead.'

The door opens and Senga climbs in the back to drop onto the seat next to me. She says hello to Murdo. I don't rate a greeting yet.

She looks at Murdo. 'We got a plan yet?'

'Aye,' I cut in, annoyed that she didn't ask me. 'We're going to kill all of—'

'Not yet,' Murdo says. 'Maybe we should go and take a look at the place first.'

I sit and sulk while Murdo drives. He pulls up across the river from the barge, and we pile out onto the street. There's no easy way to get to the barge. The path on either side of it is exposed, with no shelter, and there's an open paved space of about a hundred feet between the barge and the road. That's got to be why they like it—nobody can sneak up on them.

Unless—

'By water,' I say. 'We could get at them from the river.'

'Oh aye, son.' Murdo nods at me, looking like he agrees at first. 'You just go get your boat, and we'll row right across.'

Senga stays quiet a little longer and then points across to the open space between the barge and the road. 'We need to draw them out. Turn their advantage against them and get them onto that open bit there, where they're exposed.'

'Fire?' I say. 'We could set the boat on fire. They'll run out.'

'If we could get close enough to set the boat on fire, we wouldn't be needing to set it on fire.'

'Fair point. How's about if we sink it?'

'Same answer.'

Baws. This whole thing is difficult. And I'm getting impatient. Beth is over there, and she needs my help. Fuck it, maybe I should just swim for it. My leg's still messed up, and the river is a killer at the best of times, but we have no better plan.

Another taxi pulls up across the river, on the road nearest the barge. Two people climb out of the back, a fit woman and a weedy-looking man. They're both dressed in suits that are too sharp for them to be cops. They must be on the other side.

A man with a gun walks out from the barge to meet them. He pats them down and then leads them towards the barge. Easy as that. I guess they have an appointment. Or they're really hungry.

'I have an idea,' Senga says.

Me and Murdo both turn to her, but she stays silent. It's like she's waiting for us to ask, waiting for us to be amazed at how clever she is. Aye, right, show us the goods first—then we'll think about it.

'Murdo, you still got your gun?'

He thinks it over, then says yes. Like that's something you'd have to think about. Then again, he is old. Maybe he'd forget to wipe his arse after taking a dump. Still, though, do you forget a gun?

'It's in the glovebox.'

We pile back into the car and drive around to the front of the barge. As we climb out, Senga grabs the gun from the glovebox and waves it at us, telling us to go on ahead and play along. We walk towards the barge and the guard comes out to meet us. He looks like Che Guevara, or like that guy who played him in the film, anyway. That one with all the singing and Madonna.

Yes, I watched a musical; fuck off.

'I got a present for your boss,' Senga says to him.

He stares at us for a while, like he's trying to spot the trick. He gives Senga this weird look, then says, 'I'll need that gun.'

She starts to hand it over, but when he leans forward she hits him with it, across the head, like a fucking badass. Twice. I hear both of them, and the sound makes my own brain shake. The guy falls to the ground slowly, sliding down against the railing behind him. He's not out cold, but his eyes are looking glazed. I've seen that look plenty of times on people who've disagreed with me.

'Aye, pal.' I want to join in on the coolness. 'You just sit down a while, take a rest.'

We head on down, Senga keeping the gun on us the whole time. She's liking this. I think I would too. Wish it was the other way around. Must be fun to be the hero with the gun. At the bottom we step through the open glass doors and into the restaurant.

Gilbert's there, and so is some old guy I recognise, though I don't know from where. His face tugs at the back of my brain. Give me time, I'll find it. The two people in the suits are standing with the old guy, the woman shaking his hand. The washer lady is here too. What's-her-name, Neda. She's bent over a chair with her back to me. When she steps aside, I see Beth. She's not moving. Her head is slumped forward onto her chest, and there's blood all down her front. Too much of it. I know that much blood—I've seen it before.

My brain flashes and rocks. It goes hot and cold, and my arms tingle.

They've killed Jenny.

The bastards.

They've killed my Jenny.

Again.

I start to lose it. I can feel my head going, my gut bouncing, all the same old heat. It's like having butterflies in my stomach, except they're all on fire and really pissed off. I look again at the old man, and his face flashes younger in my mind, and I've seen him before. I've seen him here before, the last time they killed Jenny. The last time I killed Jenny. *Wait.* No. Breathe. Calm down. Think what Beth said, before she turned into Jenny.

Before.

Beth's dead.

I love Beth.

I turn to throw myself at Gilbert because he's nearest. Something hits me in the back. Hard. It knocks me to the ground, and I spit blood. What the fuck? I know this feeling. I felt it last night, and I didn't like it then, either. I've been fucking shot again. This time my back is burning. When I was shot in my leg, it was cold. I wish my body would make its fucking mind up. I roll onto my side and look up. Senga is stood over me. Murdo is lying on the floor next to me. His face is missing. When did that happen?

I hear two gunshots, but neither of them hits me. Then I hear a scream that sounds like me. My brain is catching up. It's replaying the last couple of seconds, just in case I hadn't figured out what happened. I try to kick at Senga, sweep her legs out, but I can't move. I could swear I had a body a minute ago, but now all I can feel is a tingling. Then cold. Ah, here we go—this is more like it. Am I underwater? I feel like I'm in a cold bath.

I look again at Beth.

I let her down. I didn't get to her in time, just like I didn't get to Jenny.

I want to scream. I want to cry. I want to rip every motherfucker on the planet apart with my bare hands. Instead, I laugh. It's a weird feeling, laughing without having a body.

The old man bends down and looks into my eyes.

'What's funny?' he asks.

'I'm not a monster.' I spit blood at his face.

225

Forty-Six
Sam

Andy crumbled when he saw us. It wasn't a dramatic thing—there was no explosion, but his shoulders sagged, and he looked ready to fall over. We led him out the front door and then walked a couple of blocks to a small whisky bar, somewhere that felt more neutral.

Phil went to the bar for drinks. He came back with a pint for Andy, a rum and Coke for me and a plain old Coke for himself. It sucked to be the designated driver in the middle of a crime investigation.

'Tell us what the hell is going on.'

'They're coming for you. They've already tried to do me.' He pulled back his coat to show a small red stain soaking through his T-shirt. He tried to shrug the coat off his shoulder to show more, but it was too painful. He panted a few times before continuing. 'You've got to run.'

'Yeah? Well, I'm good at running, so that's fine. But who are you talking about? The people who've killed Rab?'

He paused. I couldn't read his face. He looked to be choosing which version of the truth to tell us. Was he holding back?

He nodded. 'Yes,' he said.

'And they killed Jenny Towler too, right?'

'That I don't know. Wait.' He looked directly at me, and I could see he was remembering something. 'Senga turned up. She had some doctor with her, Mackie's psychiatrist. They were going to use her to lure Mackie. Someone said something then—I don't remember who. A lot has happened.' He touched his shoulder again. 'But someone did say something about Mackie being innocent.'

'Senga's on their side?' Shit. That changed everything. That meant Hillcoat was in trouble. And if they had Beth, I needed to do something. 'We've got to save Beth.'

Lambert shook his head. 'Don't be an idiot. How you plan to do that? You're not Rambo. Or Rambette. You walk onto that boat, and you're not coming back off again.'

I pulled my phone from my bag and waved it at him. 'Who said anything about going there myself? Which boat are they on? I'm calling the cops.'

Lambert reached across the desk and grabbed my wrist with his good arm, pulling the phone away from my face. Phil pushed between the two of us and grabbed Lambert's arm, forcing him to let go, before slamming it down onto the table. We became very conscious of other people in the bar, and the barman stopped talking to one of his customers to stare at us.

I smiled at him and shrugged an apology.

Strike one. We were on borrowed time in here. That was fine—we seemed to be on borrowed time everywhere.

'What the fuck?' Phil spat at Lambert. I'd never seen him so protective.

'Sorry.' Lambert was panting hard now, and I could see the red stain spreading beneath his jacket. 'Not thinking straight. Decisions, fuzzy. She'll already be dead. If you call the police, all you're doing is sending me down too. The people on the boat, they've set me up.

They're making it look like I killed Rab, and now that they have my blood, they can do a good job of it. I just need a little time to figure my way out of this.'

I turned the face of my phone to him to show that I'd killed the connection. I put it down on the table without letting him see that I'd pressed record on the dictation software.

'Andy,' I said. 'Start talking.'

'Rab talks too much. And with his books, it's even worse. At first he wrote about the small things, fights he'd been in, people he'd hurt. He'd stretch the truth and make himself out to be a lot harder than he was. Everyone knew it—both sides, them and us. Officers working Rab's file didn't bother reading his books sometimes because they knew there were too many lies in them.'

'But he stopped lying?'

Andy nodded and took another slow breath. 'His new book, he started writing about things he was involved in, things that he'd sworn never to tell. See, it turns out Rab liked to burn things.'

'Things?'

'Buildings. Cars. Fields. For all his tough talk in the books, what he really did, and what he made his money from, was arson. If someone was holding out on a security payment, Rab would be called in and the building would go up in smoke. If there was a listed building, something that was holding up a property deal or a large development, Rab could make that building go away.'

'That seems to happen a lot around here.'

Glasgow had long had an open secret about arson. Large parts of the South Side had vanished. Listed buildings, churches and old town halls had been standing in the way of the council being able to sell land, and the buildings all had a habit of burning down in mysterious circumstances. The crimes were never solved.

'You're not kidding.' Andy sipped his drink. 'That big church in The Gorbals? That was him. The Co-op building? Him. Property deals going back twenty or thirty years have involved his match-book. But he's just a small part of it, and when the other people got wind that he was going to write about his arson habit in his new book—'

'He became a problem. Names. Come on. Who was in this with him?'

'Well, Gilbert Neil tried to talk to him. Tried to find out what was going to be in the book and to get Rab to agree to cancel it and write some other pish instead. But he came away from that meeting yesterday and said Rab was being a dick and that he wouldn't say what was in the book but that he hadn't finished it yet.'

'So killing him now would mean killing the book.'

'Yes.'

'So I get why people would be taking shots at Rab last night, and that accounts for the mess that was cleaned up at his flat, but why would it mean someone taking shots at Mackie? How does he tie into all this?'

Andy stared at me blankly for a second.

'I, uh, don't know. Good question.'

'Andy, you're sweet when you're being an idiot. I was only really asking for effect. I don't think the people who went for Rab are the same people who went for Mackie.' I watched his eyes. They answered a few of my questions. 'How much do you guess it would cost to hire two hit men to take out someone with a violent reputation like Mackie?'

'I don't know.'

'Well, *I* guess it would take around sixty grand. Or maybe a little more than that, but perhaps Rab had the rest already and paid that up front, and the sixty was needed to pay them off when the job was done.'

Phil turned to stare at me, his expression a mix of shock and pride. 'Rab?'

'Only answer that really makes sense. Jenny was killed after she failed to get information about a property developer. Hillcoat. Yes, you know the name, right? She was Mackie's girlfriend, so she'd be known to Rab. She'd worked from school for Hillcoat's company for work experience, and then she went back full-time. Maybe Rab put her up to it. Maybe he just introduced her to someone who did. Then when she failed, they shut her up to protect their deals, and blamed Mackie.'

'Why would Rab frame his own nephew?' Phil asked. 'And why would he then want him killed?'

'Well, the second one will be easy to answer once we figure out the first. We just need to know who he felt was worth protecting more than his own family. Andy, I asked for names.'

'I can't.'

'With everything you've got on the line at this point, I'm pretty sure you can. Who's still worth protecting by now?'

He hesitated. There was something else there. I could see him still fighting back. Then he slumped in his seat and gave it up. 'Joe McLean.'

'Your father-in-law?'

'Yes. I don't know all the details. Only what he's let me know. He was always corrupt when he was on the force. He's got stories going right back to Bible John about the things they used to get away with. He saw what was going on with the property deals, and he muscled in, took over. He's been running the racket ever since.'

'And how did he drag you into it?'

'By my dick. Or my ego. Both.' He took another long pull on his drink and wiped at his lips with his thumb. 'I was a young guy with a uniform. I was getting off on being a cop, all the prestige. It was different back then. It was a club—everyone stuck together, everyone had your back. But some people seemed to live better lives than others—better houses, better booze, better holidays. Joe put his arm around me, told me he could show me how it all worked. And then I met Jess—I met his daughter, and after that it was all easy.'

He couldn't look me in the eye. I cut him some slack. It must be hard trying to talk about falling in love with your wife when you're drinking with a woman you've screwed behind the wife's back.

'So your father-in-law is the one who ordered Rab lifted?' I waited until he nodded. 'And it's a good guess that maybe he was involved in the Jenny Towler thing too. He could be the reason Rab betrayed Mackie. Maybe out of fear—who knows. I'll need to figure that out before I can prove anything.'

'You're not going to try, surely?'

I ignored that. 'Andy, what's your part in all of this. Just how involved are you?'

'I know about the arson and the property deals. I keep an eye on the police investigations. There are guys like me at the council too, people who make sure it all works the right way.'

'And Rab's murder?'

He took too long to answer, and something inside me died. He was in this up to his neck. And I'd let the slimy fucker get up close and personal with me. I felt sick, but I held it back. I needed to keep him talking. I imagined I was playing poker—I didn't want him to see that I'd got his cards marked.

'I didn't know about that,' he said. 'I swear. Me and Jess, we've been planning to run away, leave. That's why I came here tonight. I was going to make a grab for the money and use it to get away.'

'You had Rab's phone.'

The wheels turned behind his eyes. It was a master class in watching someone lie.

'Yes,' he nodded. 'Like I said, they've tried to set me up. I started asking questions about Rab. I figured out what had happened, and they didn't like it. One of their guys beat me up, took me to where his body is and tried to kill me too. They put my blood at the scene, wanted it to look like it was all down to me.'

I risked a look at my phone. The screen had gone dark, but I trusted that the app was still recording. It wouldn't be catching the look in his eyes, the telltale signs, but it would be a good starting point.

I could push it home now. He was hurt and not thinking straight, and it would be easy enough to trip him into a real admission, but I needed something else first.

'And my dad. How does he figure into all this?'

He smiled.

'Your old man figured all this out a long time ago. Part of some other case he was working. He got it all and had proof.'

'What happened next?'

'He made a deal.'

Forty-Seven
Lambert

Lambert hated having to lie to Sam. She was one of the good guys, and he was really fond of her. But he needed to build a way out of this. They'd caught him red-handed with Rab's phone, coming for money that only Rab and Gaz would have known was waiting there, and it was important they believed him. It might buy him the time he needed to get back to Jess and leave town.

They did believe him. Lambert could feel it. He could see Sam was hesitant, but in her eyes she was buying what he was saying. He knew her well enough to see that. Phil? He was more of a mystery. Lambert had never slept with him, so he didn't have any understanding to go on, but Phil was nodding in all the right places.

'Your old man figured all this out a long time ago,' Lambert said. He saw a flash in Sam's eyes. 'Part of some other case he was working. He got it all and had proof.'

'What happened next?'

'He made a deal,' Lambert said.

Here he was on solid ground. He could tell the truth about all this because he didn't really know much about it, and there was nothing to incriminate him. Sam and Phil reacted differently.

Sam nodded. She'd already been figuring out that her old man was involved somehow. Phil got angry. A young boy being told his hero father might not have been all hero. Lambert kept his eyes on Sam because she was the one talking to him, but he was keeping track of Phil's reactions. Fatso looked like he was building to something.

'What kind of deal?'

Sam was holding her voice level. Keeping emotions in check.

'Your dad had tapes, I think. Something, anyway. Something he could hold over Joe. But he knew it was all too big for him. As good as he was, and as connected as he was, he was just a PI. And he had a family. A single dad with two kids? He had to make the deal.'

Phil leant in. 'She asked you what kind of deal.' He almost spat as he spoke.

'You two. That was the deal. He would back off, and the evidence would go away, and he would always be allowed to work in the city, and you two would always be safe. That's why you've lasted so long today, Sam. They've been holding back, trying to stick to the deal, but they've decided enough is enough. When they find you, they'll kill you.'

Sam nodded and smiled. Lambert loved the reaction. She was every bit her dad now, a full-on private investigator. 'So where's his evidence?' she asked.

'What?' Lambert and Phil asked at the same time.

'Well, for that deal to have worked, and for it to have lasted as long as it has, he has to have been holding it over them, as you said. They have to believe that the evidence could be released at any time.'

'Sam.' Phil talked in a low voice, as if Lambert wouldn't hear it. 'You checked the files. There's nothing there.'

'Exactly,' Sam said. 'It has to be somewhere safe. Secure. Because Joe doesn't have it either, otherwise he wouldn't still be worried about it. The evidence is out there somewhere.'

Damn. She was right. For Joe to have been backing off all this time meant that old Jim Ireland had put it somewhere safe. Somewhere protected. And if it was still out there to be found, it was also still out there to be used. One last roll of the dice for Lambert. If he could find the proof before anyone else, he could use it the same way Jim Ireland had done.

Lambert and Jess wouldn't need to run and hide like teenagers. They could make a deal with Joe, walk away on their own terms.

'Where do you think it is?' Lambert tried not to sound too interested as he asked. Playing it casual. Playing it cool. Playing it like he didn't have a giant stab wound in his shoulder.

Sam sat in silence, sipping from her drink. She watched Lambert over the top of her glass. Phil was still simmering. He had the whole male pride thing going on. Even though he knew that what had been said about his dad was true, he still needed to lash out. Lambert waited for Sam to finish drinking. He knew she was thinking.

'I'll find it.' Sam placed her glass back on the table. 'Me and Phil. Who killed Rab?'

Lambert's mouth opened and closed. He coughed into his drink. He hadn't been expecting the sudden change in gears. 'What?'

'Don't treat us like idiots. You're trying to talk your way out. Aye, all right, I've let you have a run at it. But why the hell would they be trying to set you up for murder? Why go to all that trouble for a body that hasn't been found and a crime that hasn't been reported?'

'I don't know. Desperate people do crazy things.'

Sam stared at Lambert. He realised how badly he'd judged the situation. He couldn't read her at all. She leant forward. 'Were you there when Rab got taken? Were you at his flat? Have you had that dog bite looked at?'

Lambert looked at his hand, where his second bandage of the day was in bad shape after the fight with Nick. 'Sam, honest, you've got this wrong.'

Lambert reached out to touch her arm, but Phil blocked him again and slammed the outstretched hand on the table. Both men jumped up, ready to challenge each other, but even as Lambert's blood rose, he knew he wasn't in a fit state to fight. His shoulder threw him a friendly shot of pain as a reminder. The barman pressed up against the edge of the counter and shouted for them to behave or leave, and both Phil and Lambert put their hands up to show that they were calm.

Lambert had knocked Sam's phone in the tussle, and it had activated the screen. He saw numbers ticking away, a timer counting upwards, and a big red light. A recorder. She'd been taping the whole thing. Their eyes met, and they both knew what he'd seen. They held the gaze for a brief moment before Lambert made a grab for the phone. Sam had seen it coming and scooped the phone out of the way.

The barman shouted again, and this time there was no final warning; he was ordering them out. Lambert was already up and running. He'd been set up by both sides and had no friends left to turn to. But there was one man who would know for sure where the evidence was buried.

He still had one play.

Forty-Eight
Sam

So my dad had figured it all out. He'd found proof. Something that was concrete enough to scare McLean, something he'd been able to use to get a deal out of them. What was it? More important, *where* was it? He wouldn't have handed it over, and these days he probably didn't even remember having it. There had been nothing in his files, unless I'd been searching for the wrong thing. But it wasn't safe for me to go back to the flat for another look.

Before I could deal with that, though, I had something else to do.

Hillcoat was a sitting duck. He wouldn't even know it. Senga had betrayed him, and he needed to be warned. Phil drove while I stressed. I only broke the silence to offer directions. We got lost twice. It was the problem with being a pedestrian; I could get pretty much anywhere on foot, but in a car I lost all sense of direction.

In less than a day I'd gone from not really wanting to be a private investigator to having the kinds of hunches my dad used to talk about after an exciting case.

I'd known Andy was lying.

I'd known Rab had been taken.

And as we pulled up outside Hillcoat's house, I knew something was wrong.

It wasn't so much a hunch as a warning. I wasn't being drawn in to investigate deeper; I was being told to run away. There was nothing magic about it. Our brains are constantly taking in details. Most of the time we don't know about it until they've been processed, turned into some complete whole. In the case of danger, though, I think our brains spit the information straight out to us, giving us the rush of adrenalin or the hairs that stand up on the backs of our necks. Somewhere deep down I'd noticed that the gate was open, whereas it had been kept closed on my first visit. The front door wasn't fully shut, and every light in the building seemed to be on, shining out like a bright beacon, daring people to look at it. And more than all of that, the signal I would most regret ignoring was the sound of police sirens in the distance.

I ignored them all and stepped in through the front door.

There was a scratching sound coming from upstairs. With Phil close in behind me, begging me to turn around and leave with him, I climbed the staircase. Halfway up, Phil put a hand on my arm and stopped me.

'Look,' he said, pointing a few steps ahead.

The outline of a branded running shoe was pressed into the carpet, a footprint etched in the dark burgundy of drying blood. The print was facing towards us, in the manner of someone running down the stairs. The scratching sound came again, and I pressed on. Phil didn't move. He stayed halfway up the stairs trying not to look scared. I stepped onto the landing and paced quietly along the carpeted floor. I walked past the room that Hillcoat had shown me before. The door was open, and I could see that all the photographs had been taken off the wall, and the documents were all gone from the desk.

The scratching was coming from further along the hall, behind a large door at the end. I touched the wood of the door for a second, trying to decide what to do. The scratching was low down, at the base of the door, and it was accompanied by a sniffing that increased as I drew near. I heard the frantic whining of a dog.

Bobby.

I opened the door, and he ran past me, along the hallway and then down the stairs. He didn't stop to inspect Phil, who yelped as the furry brown blur raced by him. I turned and looked back into the room. I was becoming accustomed to the smell of blood, and it didn't turn my stomach as I stepped into the room and saw a trail of it across the floor. There were two large lumps of meat on the bed. I took a couple of paces closer, enough to make out the blood-streaked faces of Hillcoat and Beth. The sounds around me snapped into focus. Phil called my name from somewhere behind me as the sound of the police sirens now filled the air. Red and blue lights strafed the room from the large window, and car doors slammed shut.

On the floor below I heard the front door crash open, and the police started calling out, warning of their arrival. I stepped back out into the hallway and looked down at Phil, who was raising his hands above his head. I followed suit and started trying to get my story straight in my mind.

Forty-Nine
Lambert

Lambert climbed over the locked gates of the care home. The grounds between him and the building were blanketed in darkness. In the summer it stayed relatively light even at this time of the evening, but the darkness was enough to keep him hidden unless he made any sudden moves. The elderly residents had been in bed for hours, and the day staff had gone home. With the gates locked, they switched the lights off in the car park and gardens.

Lambert had visited the home once before, on a call-out for a robbery, and had told the managers that they should keep the exterior lights on after curfew. This was one time he was glad his advice had been ignored. He caught another movement in the grounds and saw a shape heading his way. It formed into a tubby security guard. The gates had rattled as Lambert climbed them, and he guessed the sound had drawn the guard.

Tubby walked straight past Lambert, who was ten feet away on the grass and holding his breath. Lambert fought the urge to squat down while Tubby inspected the gate, because any movement might give him away in the grey night air. Instead, he stayed still and held his breath as the guard finished his inspection and walked back in the direction of the building, dissolving into the shadows as he rounded the far corner and walked on.

Lambert remembered that Jim Ireland's room was at the rear of the building, overlooking the lawn, but it was on the first floor, and Lambert wouldn't be able to climb up. He needed to get inside the building first. The large wooden door at the front of the building was locked. He risked a look in through the window to the side of the door and saw two members of staff at a reception desk, flicking through magazines and holding a stilted conversation. The door itself looked like a heavy-duty operation. It probably stayed locked all night, which meant the guard would come and go through a different entrance. Lambert headed off in the direction the guard had taken.

Around the corner was another stretch of wall, with more parking spaces to the right. Lambert pressed on, walking as quietly as he could, and passed beneath an archway that connected the old building to a more recent extension, out of sight from the road. Soon he saw the shape of the guard again, walking slowly away from him, occasionally whistling some tone-deaf tune. Half of it sounded like a football standard; half of it sounded like a broken nose.

Lambert picked up his pace as he got more confident, sure enough of himself that the guard wouldn't hear him and wanting to be close enough to see the combination to a door or to stop it shutting after the guard stepped in. Once he was within five feet of the guard, the whistling stopped. The guard coughed and then spun on his heels. Lambert was close enough now that he could see the guard smile.

'This the guy?' the guard said.

He wasn't speaking to Lambert.

'That's him.' Joe McLean stepped out from the side of the extension. Gilbert Neil followed suit from the other side, the way Lambert had come. 'Good work, Tommy. Andy, keep your fucking hands where I can see them, aye?' Joe produced a gun. 'I'd really rather not use it. Gunshots attract attention.'

Joe pointed for Lambert to keep going in the direction he'd been headed, and the guard led the way. They walked along the building in silence, with Lambert trying to think of his next move, and then through an archway at the other end of the extension, onto a path that led through the overhanging trees.

Joe raised his voice to speak to the guard, who was a couple of feet ahead of Lambert. 'Tommy, how's your ma doing?'

'Oh aye.' Tommy turned back and nodded. 'She's fine, thanks, Mr McLean. The new hip's worked out well for her. She likes it so much she wants to get the other done.'

'And your old man—he still working in his allotment?'

'Aye, down there every night, so he is. Can't complain. I get some pure good homebrew out of it—he does great things with sprouts.'

'Sprouts? Can't abide them. They're like snot on a plate. Ever since I was a wee boy, I've had a thing about them.'

'So I shouldn't bring you any of his sprout beer at Christmas, then?'

'Best not.' Joe was talking like a friendly old man, and Lambert felt like laughing at the absurdity of it all. 'Well, thanks for your help, Tommy.' Joe handed him an envelope as they came out of the trees on the other side. 'Give my best to Rosa.'

'Will do, sir.'

The guard headed away, back the way they had come, whistling the tuneless tune again.

They were standing on a field at the far end of the care home's grounds. The grass had been ripped up in this corner, and there were mounds of soil and some freshly planted trees. Ahead of them was a hill made out of stone circles and soil, heading up in layers to a peak. Next to the hill was a large round pit, big enough to fit in a couple of cars side by side.

'Landscaping,' Joe said. 'This whole bit is going to look great when it's done. We'll put a pond in there, on top of you, and a small water-fall can come down the hill. A few benches where we're stood. Perfect little garden for the old folks to come and sit in the summer, read books or whatever.'

'People will look for me.'

Gilbert snorted. 'Not here they won't.'

Lambert looked down at the dirt at his feet, then at the grass and debris around him. Somewhere in all the mess he hoped to see a weapon. A spade, a hoe, anything large enough. He needed to stall for time until he could figure something out.

'How did you know I was coming?'

'Once we figured out you'd killed Nick we asked around. You were spotted talking to Sam in the Nevis Bar, and she's been arrested at Hillcoat's house, so I figured you might try here. It's the only play you have left.'

'Why?'

'Because Jim Ireland is here. Don't make me have to explain what you already know.'

'But how did you know Jim was here? I only know because I came here on a call-out once, saw him.'

'I own the place, dum-dum.' Joe was laughing but there was no smile on his lips. 'How else do you think the fees would be afford-able to the Ireland family? I arranged a discount for them years ago, keeping him looked after.'

'Keeping an eye on him, you mean.'

'Sure, that too.'

'Because you don't know where his evidence is.'

'You really want to do this? Okay. Fine, yes, because of the evi-dence. It's not going to be a problem much longer, though. I've found a good lawyer, and after tonight all the loose ends will be tied up.'

Lambert stopped scanning the ground and stared at Joe. The tone in his voice said he had all his bases covered. There had been a hint of nervousness to him at the house and on the boat, but it had gone. He knew his way out of the situation now, and Joe was good at coming out on the winning side. That made something inside Lambert die. Maybe it was hope.

'You've spoken to Fiona Hunter?'

'I have. And her partner. They've pointed out that if Jim Ireland set up the evidence to be released in the event of his death, and it's something his daughter didn't know about, then it's going to be tied up in his will. All we need to do is get to the executor of his will and we're free and clear.'

'Sam?'

Joe nodded. 'Uh-huh. Or Phil, the son. Or if it's not either of them, they'll know who it is. So we get to them, we get to the will, we solve the problem.'

'But you said Sam was arrested?'

'We threw a little party at Hillcoat's house. The police are never going to come looking for us now—they have no reason to. All the dead bodies can be explained. Sam got there just before the police, which worked out well for us. We'd been trying to figure out a way to get her, and she fell into our laps.'

'But if she's in jail, you'll need me to—'

Joe shook his head once and then raised the gun in the space between them, pointing it at Lambert's face. 'No,' he said. 'Like I said. We have a good lawyer now. And we have a deal. Show of commitment from both parties. They're going to take care of the Ireland kids, and we're going to take care of you. No more loose ends.'

Lambert took a couple steps backwards—putting an extra two feet of distance between him and the gun, which would make no difference at all. He felt the earth slip at his heels and turned to see he was on the edge of the pit.

He tried to think.

Options.

Options.

Just one fucking option, please.

'You said you didn't want to use a gun,' he said.

Joe hesitated. He lowered the gun. 'You're right,' he said.

Lambert saw hope. He went in for one last play.

'Please. Jess is pregnant. We're having a baby.'

Joe took a step back and turned to Gilbert. They smiled at each other, and Gilbert patted him on the back.

'You hear that, Gil? I'm going to be a grandda.'

'Aye, well in, Joe. Congratulations, big man.'

'I hope his stepdad is better than the real thing.'

Joe turned back towards Lambert. There was an odd sound, like metal sliding out of metal. Joe waved something in front of Lambert's face. Lambert coughed. His throat was wet, phlegmy like a cold. He felt water running down his neck. Joe held a knife up in the space between them and smiled. Joe touched his hand to his throat and felt the blood running between his fingers, the air sucking through the wound. He staggered backwards. His last thought was *It's probably okay to feel squeamish right now.*

Fifty
Sam

My dad used to brag about how many times he'd been arrested. It was a point of pride for him. Each one, as far as he was concerned, was an occasion when he'd been better at his job than the cops were at theirs. A time when he'd got to a scene before them or found a clue they'd missed. He'd tell stories about each of them, and his voice would crack with mischief as a smile flicked the corner of his mouth.

But it was a new experience for me.

They'd taken me to the big police station on Helen Street. This was where they'd interrogated the suspects in the airport terrorist attack and where the Prime Minister's communications expert had turned himself in over the phone-hacking scandal. I allowed myself to feel a wee bit like a celebrity as they led me in through the door. They'd separated Phil and me at the house. They'd been rougher on him as they arrested us. His size made people nervous, and they overcompensated. He'd been bundled into the first car that pulled up, the one in the driveway, while I was led out to a car waiting in the road.

In the station I was booked in, my possessions were taken and I was led straight into an interrogation room and left on my own.

Or I assumed it was an interrogation room, anyway. It was a room—that much I was comfortable with. There was a table in the middle, with two plastic chairs on each side. But there was also a sofa pushed against a wall, and a water cooler in the corner. There were pictures on the wall, with photographs of old Glasgow buildings.

Was this how they got the terrorists to crack, by being nice to them? It was pretty cunning. I helped myself to a cup of chilled water and sat on the sofa, leaning back into the imitation leather. When the two police officers walked in, they both smiled at me and nodded at where I was sitting.

'Comfortable?' asked the older cop. He was middle-aged and mostly bald. 'I like that spot too.'

'Mind if we join you?' The other cop was an Asian woman. She was younger and looked like she worked out. Her suit was cheap, like a Primark special, but who was I to judge?

I held my hands out to say, sure, why not? 'It's your place,' I said. 'I'm just the guest.'

They both smiled at this. The woman sat down beside me, leaving a proper amount of space between us, showing she was well trained, while the man pulled over one of the plastic chairs from the table and sat in front of me.

'Sam,' he said. 'Can I call you Sam? Knew your father. He was a good cop. A better detective. We should have promoted him, not let him go. And the lad in the other room, the one who keeps talking about wrestling and comics, that's your wee brother, right?'

'Aye.' I nodded. He was being nice, and it was unnerving.

'Sorry, I forgot the introductions. I'm John Cummings. This is Hanya Perera. She's English, but don't hold it against her.'

247

'I'll try.'

Perera smiled at that. 'We'd like to talk to you about what happened at the house,' she said.

I looked from one to the other, then over at the empty table. There was something missing from every film and television scene I'd seen. 'Shouldn't we be recording this? I mean, for evidence?'

Cummings waited a second. He leant back and pulled a digital recorder from the inside pocket of his jacket. 'Sure, if you like.'

'The thing is,' Perera leant in closer and talked quietly, like she was sharing gossip, 'I think you'd be better off just talking to us for a while before we do all of that.'

What the hell, I'd hear them out. I'd been found in a house I didn't own, stood next to two dead bodies. I decided I could afford to take a few risks.

'Listen to this.' Cummings pressed a few buttons of the digital device and then a recording started to play. It was a call to the emergency services, recorded from the receiving end. I recognised the conversation straight away, because it was the one I'd had earlier. It was a copy of the anonymous tip I'd called in about the Copland Road house. Why were they letting me listen to it off the record?

'I find this interesting,' Cummings said. 'I'm sure we wouldn't have a hard time proving that this is your voice. Or that we wouldn't have a hard time proving it just enough to make a case, at any rate.'

'Go on.'

'And it was a tip about a brothel. Yes, we know what it was. We'd be pretty bad at our jobs if we hadn't known about the place, right? The property's in the name of Robert Anderson. When our colleagues got there, the place was on fire, but the fire service did a good enough job that we could tell there was a lot of blood at the scene. Blood, but no body.'

I didn't answer, but my silence also lacked any denial. I was going to keep following, see where this led.

Perera took up the story. 'And a short while ago, we received another anonymous call—no idea who made it at the moment—that led us to the home of Ryan Hillcoat, whom we found dead, along with Dr Elizabeth Carter, a colleague of many people in this building.'

'Hillcoat's name is on a watch list,' Cummings said. 'I have a few special projects. Open files on certain individuals and certain crimes. When the call came in, it flashed up from my list. Any other day, I'd have been the first one to the scene. But at the time I was already attending a crime scene. Someone dumped two bodies in a lock-up in The Gorbals and torched them. You sensing a pattern here?' He mimed explosions with his two hands and made a brief whooshing noise. 'We have a house set alight that has blood, but no body. We have a lock-up set alight that has two bodies, but no murder weapon. And then this thing with Hillcoat.'

I played ignorant. 'So?'

'We spoke to Dr Carter earlier today. She was visiting the same patient as us in hospital, someone who later escaped.'

'Malcolm Jack Mackie,' Perera said.

I've never been very good at poker. The name must have triggered a brief reaction in my face, because I saw them both notice it.

'Mackie had a bullet wound,' Cummings said. 'In his leg. So that's another crime without a weapon. But he's known for cutting people up. Famous for it, really. And we have a whole lot of blood, and three out of the four bodies are people who've been cut up.'

'And Mackie himself,' Perera leant in again. 'He's nowhere to be found.'

I looked from one to the other. I clicked my fingers and pointed at each of them. 'You've practised this, haven't you. The whole back-and-forth thing. You're doing it well. Slick.'

I could see how they were piecing it all together, though. Some-one was doing a very good job of tying the whole mess up into a neat trail that led right to Mackie. They'd got away with pinning a murder on him before, and it was simple to do it again. But how did I fit into all of this?

'You want me to fill in the blanks?'

'Maybe.' Cummings stood up and walked over to the table. He placed the recorder in the middle. 'If you have anything we can use to fill them. Look, Sam, I like you. I liked your dad. You and I both know you didn't kill anyone. You've been working a case and got mixed up in this. We have enough circumstantial evidence to make your life difficult for a while, but why would we want to do that? We can work together on this.'

'This is how we think it can work.' Perera stood up and joined him on the other side of the table. She pointed to the empty chair opposite them. 'When we start the official interview, trust us. Let us guide you through, and give us answers to the questions we ask, and we can all go home at the end. Do we have a deal?'

I joined them at the table and eased into the empty seat. The easy thing to do, the common sense thing to do, was to play whatever game they wanted and then go home free to a warm bed. Let them patronise me and control me, and help them set up an innocent man.

But I couldn't go home to a warm bed because the real killers knew where I lived. And if I helped them all get away with it, I'd be doing their job for them and setting myself up to quietly disappear.

And to top it all off, these smug fuckers thought they could use memories of my dad as a way to manipulate me.

'How it will work,' I said, 'is *the law*. You're going to follow it. I'm going to answer questions. And it's going to take however long it takes. Now, I think you should stop messing around and start the actual interview. One thing, though, before you do? Go and get my phone from the locker. There's a recording on it that I think should be part of our interview.'

An icy silence dropped between us. They stared at the table, then at their hands, then at each other. Neither of them looked at me. Cummings drummed his fingers on the table and then turned and nodded at Perera.

'Fine.' Perera walked over to the door. She left the room, and the temperature at the table dropped even further.

'I hope you've not got any plans for tomorrow morning,' Cummings said. 'Because we may have to hold you overnight for the full questioning.'

Fine. At least Phil and I would be safe behind bars. That was one way of getting through the night. It would give me plenty of time to think about where Dad would have hidden the evidence. Did he have a bank vault? No, surely I would have been told about that when I got power of attorney. I was given access to all of his accounts and personal details. Fran had made sure of that.

Fran, my dad's solicitor.

My solicitor.

Crap.

Of course. That was who had the evidence. If I'd used my brain, I would have figured it out as soon as Andy mentioned it existed. But I was new at this whole detection thing, and I decided after a day of figuring everything out, I was allowed a mistake.

The door opened again, and Perera stepped back in. She waved my phone at me and then nodded for Cummings to join her outside. Cummings gave me a look that said, *Don't you fucking move.* Then he stepped out into the hall and pulled the door behind him. They didn't shut the door fully, so I could hear muted conversation, without being able to make out the details.

As the door started to push inwards again, I heard Cummings say, 'Who told her?'

They then both turned to face me. Cummings opened the door wide.

'Your solicitor is here to sit in on the interview.'

'My solicitor?'

Fiona Hunter walked in.

Fifty-One

Fiona made short work of Cummings and Perera. She scolded them like a schoolteacher, and they admitted that they didn't wish to keep me and that they would be very grateful if I could provide them with a statement. They even said *please*. We listened to the recording, with them taping the process on the digital recorder. I already knew the information on the tape. I'd already spent the day piecing things together and being surprised by what I found. I made a great sport out of watching the reactions of the three people sitting with me as they heard the recording for the first time.

Fiona cocked her head occasionally and made a few low interested sounds, like she'd been given a new fact in a pub quiz. Cummings and Perera didn't seem surprised. If anything, it looked like most of it confirmed ideas they'd already had. It was when we got to the bit about Mackie being innocent that the cops showed a new emotion. They stared at each other, and Perera reached for the notepad that she'd stopped pretending to use earlier in the recording.

'Go back,' Cummings said. 'Play that bit over.'

I flipped the timeline of the recording back a few seconds and let it start playing again. Cummings let his eyes grow wider with each passing word, until I thought his face was going to vanish from sight behind them.

'I worked that case,' he said, managing to sound deflated and inspired at the same time. 'Mackie doesn't remember me, but I'm the one who arrested him. He looked like a wee boy. If I hadn't found him over her, if he hadn't been covered in her blood—'

Perera nudged him. 'Not on the recording,' she said.

Cummings reached out and paused the digital recorder.

'This is going to be huge, if we can crack it. A retired cop, a serving officer, one of Glasgow's most famous murder cases and a property scam that implicates the council. It'll either make our careers or end them. If we can find a way to use any of this.'

I didn't understand. 'Find a way?'

'We can't build a case around this. It's a recording made by a civilian, with no video footage, and everything in it is hearsay. McLean's solicitors would cut it down before it got even a whiff of going to court.'

'Our bosses would never agree to it.' Perera nodded along. 'We may not be able to do anything based on this alone.'

'Do they know that?' Fiona spoke up for the first time since the tape started playing. 'These men that are named in the tape. Joe McLean, Gilbert Neil. The one speaking is a cop, I assume? Okay. And one of them used to be a cop. But does that mean you couldn't trick him into a confession?'

'We could use this recording as enough for an arrest, if we ask nicely,' Cummings said.

He pressed record on the digital device again and then nodded for me to restart the audio. I pulled it back again to where it had been when the interruption had started. We listened to the whole thing, right up to when Andy had tried to make a grab for the device, where the recording stopped.

'What happened at the end of the recording there? It just cut out?'

'Yes. Andy—Lambert—he realised I was taping him and did a runner. He seemed pretty desperate at that point, and he looked injured. I'm not sure how badly, but he probably needed treatment. Also, I think he was the one who lifted Rab from his flat, or was part of a team that did it, though I couldn't get him to say so on the tape.'

'What makes you think that?'

'I broke—um, *visited* Rab's flat myself earlier today. If you go there, you'll probably find a few of my prints. Anyway, Rab owned a dog, but there was no sign of it, and someone had used a lot of bleach. I reckon the dog tried to attack them, maybe defending Rab, and they had to kill it.'

'And?'

'Andy's been wearing a bandage on his hand all day. Except he'd taken it off by the time we were talking to him on the tape. He said he'd done it at home, but the wound looked a lot like a dog bite to me. You could practically see the teeth marks. And whoever killed Hillcoat and Beth didn't kill Bobby, the wee dog, so it was someone different.'

'Interesting work, Sherlock. But something else that's not really going to help us.' Cummings scratched his chin, cupping it with his hand while he thought. It made a sound like sandpaper. 'This pretty much confirms the two dead bodies we found in the lock-up in The Gorbals.' Cummings turned to Perera. 'And we can make educated guesses about what happened to Hillcoat and Carter. Killed to make it look like Mackie, see if they can pull the same trick on me twice. But how do we make a case?'

Perera announced the time and those in attendance, and then reached over to stop the device from recording. 'Ms Hunter may be right,' she said. 'We can maybe get a confession off the back of it. Lean on Gilbert; roll him into McLean.'

'If I may, there is another option.' Fiona tapped the table idly with her forefinger, drawing everyone's attention to her. '*Entrapment* is a dirty word. But I've never seen a crime that can't be solved by catching someone in the act. Just speaking as a concerned citizen, of course, because this will not implicate my client in any way.'

Cummings stared at her; the wheels were spinning behind his eyes. 'Go on.'

'Well, there's the matter of the missing evidence. If word got out about its location. I'm sure my client has figured out where it is by now.'

All three of them turned to me and waited. I'd been holding onto this through the interview, waiting to see if there was a best time to use my get-out-of-jail-free card—the moment when I might need it to pull myself out of trouble or to seal a deal that was being made.

I nodded. 'I know where it is.'

Cummings and Perera shared a silent moment and then left the room together to confer.

Fiona turned in her chair to face me. 'You've had quite a day,' she said.

'You can say that again. And you, you're quite the schemer. All that stuff you just did, you try that for every client?'

'Just the ones I like. You've impressed us. You and your brother. We hire you to serve a few simple papers, and you bring a whole conspiracy down around us. Corruption. Fire raising. Murder. They're going to be talking about this for years. They're going to be wanting to talk to *you* for years.'

She smiled. It was a smile that came with more than one tone. She was humouring me, patronising me and sizing me up all at the same time. I thought back to what Fran had said about her breed of solicitor, wanting to work celebrity cases to make their names. I'd just landed her the golden ticket.

'But speaking of my brother,' I said, 'is someone in with him?'

'Yes, my partner, Douglas, is in with him now. When we're done, the two of you should come back to our place. We'll get some food in, some wine, and talk about our future.'

'*Our* place?'

'Yes, mine and my partner's.'

The penny didn't so much drop as lower itself slowly into view in my brain, before the cord was cut and it crashed down into a pile of other moments of stupidity. 'Oh, I see. Douglas is your *partner*. Right. Don't take this the wrong way, but I'd thought you were—'

'We get that a lot. But we're married. We kept our separate names, and it helps with the firm's name—gives off a different impression. But I notice you picked up on that bit but ignored the part where I mentioned us having a future.'

I hadn't ignored it at all, but I wanted to play it cool. The way my dad would have done, with an easy nod and a non-committal gesture, pretend like it didn't mean the whole world.

'I was just playing it cool,' I said, ignoring everything I'd thought about. 'Pretend like it didn't mean the world.'

It was time to stop playing at being my dad and start being myself. For the first time, though, I could see a version of myself that wanted to be doing this job. A version of myself that liked the chase and the adrenalin, that liked putting together the clues and making mental leaps of logic.

Cummings and Perera stepped back into the room.

'We're on,' Cummings said. 'If you'll agree to it, Sam?'

'Aye.'

Who needs Philip Marlowe?

Fifty-Two

I knew that package was trouble. Always knew. If it had been any-one else, I would have said no. But your old man, I couldn't let him down.'

Fran was seated on the sofa across from me in my living room. He was wearing a large woollen housecoat. Beneath it I caught a glimpse of flannel pyjamas; he'd pulled a pair of jeans on over the trousers. His hair waved across his scalp like an explosion, and his beard was sticking out at funny angles. He looked like a bear that had been woken from hibernation too early. His arms were folded across his chest, and he was staring at a brown manila package shaped like a brick that was sitting on my coffee table.

Until around fifteen minutes earlier, it had been taking up space in his safe.

I'd called him from the police station, a chance to run up their phone bill rather than mine, and given a brief explanation of what was going on. As soon as I'd mentioned my dad's name, I'd heard him chuckle. He said he'd been wondering when I would call. He agreed to meet us at the office in half an hour, which then started a long debate among Cummings, Perera and Fiona.

'My client is certainly not going to the scene with you while armed criminals are on their way there.' Fiona stood in front of both cops, staring them down. 'And I'm not comfortable with you leaving her here until we've worked out if Lambert is the only dirty cop in on this.'

'Listen, love. I mean—' He faltered under an icy stare from Fiona. 'Ms Hunter. The cop who denies some of his colleagues are corrupt is the cop who *is* corrupt. It happens in every walk of life. But it would be safer if—'

'It would be safer for us to not do this at all. But since my client is cooperating and allowing you to use her as bait in a trap, you will play by our rules.'

Our rules, she'd said, as if I'd been playing a part in planning this. I just sat back and watched. She was pretty fearsome when she needed to be. Cummings threw his hand up in the air theatrically and then turned to face the wall while he calmed down and thought things through.

'Okay, okay, fine. Sam can go home. But I want people with her.'

'Naturally, one of you two will accompany us.' *Us?* 'And you will have an armed officer outside, just in case.'

Cummings and Perera took it in turns to stare at Fiona like she'd just taken a dump on their shoes, then at each other like she'd just asked if they had any bog paper. Then Perera made the decision.

'I used to be in the old Armed Response Team before the forces merged. I transferred out to CID. I can do both—I'll sit with you, and I can sign out a gun. It'll take me a while to clear that, though, so you better get comfortable.'

'Oh jeez-o,' Cummings spoke under his breath, and then to the room. 'We'll be filling in paperwork until I take my pension.'

It took another forty minutes, which gave time for me to get in touch with Fran again and ask him to meet us at my place instead

259

of the office. Cummings and Perera took it in turns to brief me on the details of what was going to happen, and Fiona made a few hushed phone calls. The tension ramped up with each attempt by any of them to tell me to relax. I was handed a number they said was Joe McLean's mobile. It was important that the call come from my phone. I typed it in and pressed delete, then did the same again, then typed it in and stared at it for five minutes. I swallowed a load of air and pressed to dial the number.

'Aye?' He answered straight away. He was out of breath but sounded wide awake.

The minute I heard his voice, my nerves went away. I was too busy being angry at everything this man had done and at all the years' worth of guilt that my dad must have been carrying around. Was it any wonder his brain gave out on him and that his memory decided it didn't want to remember anything? It may have had no scientific backing, but in that moment Joe McLean was the reason for my father's illness.

'I gather you're looking for me.'

'Am I?'

'I'll be at Crowther's. You know where it is?'

'Aye.'

'And you know what they do?'

'I do.'

'So you'll know why I'm there. Come and make me a good offer. I want out of this game.'

Perera drove Phil, Fiona and me to my flat, where Fran was already waiting in his car. Phil made himself busy getting tea and coffee for everyone while Perera hovered by the window like a caged animal waiting for the latch to spring open. I brought Fran up to speed on the whole story.

He placed the package on the table and then eased back into the sofa.

'I wish you'd taken the divorce case,' he said. 'I knew that package was trouble. Always knew. If it had been anyone else, I would have said no. But your old man, I couldn't let him down.'

He settled back into his seat and crossed his arms over his chest, staring at the package.

'Do you know what's in it?' I said.

'No. Never wanted to. One day Jim asked me to keep it safe and never to tell anyone. A while later he updated his will, gave me instructions on where to send the evidence when he died. Then you got power of attorney, and that meant I was going to leave the decision to you. You know, when the time comes.'

I stood up and walked over to the table, running my hand across the top of the package. This thing had kept me alive and kept my dad working, right up till his health had got the better of him. How much must it have taken out of him to make the deal? How much of his own pride had he locked away in that safe?

'Don't open that.' Perera stepped forward and put a hand out, still a few feet away from me, but making the intent clear. 'That's police evidence.'

'Bollocks it is. Whatever it is, it's my dad's, and it's mine, and I'll turn it over to you once I've had a look.'

Phil handed me a pair of scissors from the kitchen, and I ripped through the paper. There were three or four layers, each one wrapped tight with parcel tape. Once the final layer came off I found a shoebox, crushed and warped into a smaller size by all the tape that had been surrounding it. The box was filled with papers and photographs, and full case files compiled by my dad. Some of the documents were typed on his old typewriter, the square inked letters that I remembered running my hands over as a little girl, when his files had seemed so exciting to me. Some were written in his neat block handwriting. There were others written in a hand I didn't recognise, a young and feminine swirling pattern in faded blue ink. The photographs were a mix of grainy printouts from old-fashioned CCTV, a world removed from the quality we could get today, and glossy Polaroids that must have been from his own surveillance. In the centre of the bundle lay a Dictaphone and three tapes. I slipped the first one in and pressed play.

'Why'd you kill her, Joe?' My father came out loud and clear above background noise. I heard the striking of a snooker ball. 'Why'd you kill the Towler girl?'

I choked a little as I heard my dad's voice. This was as I wanted to remember him, young and strong, confident. There was a steel and a comfort in his words that you couldn't fake, and they'd all faded from the old man I visited at 4.00 p.m. most days. Phil stepped to my side and put a hand on my shoulder.

'Had to. She'd set us up. Rab's fault.' Joe's voice was slurred with alcohol and bravado. He was drunk and showing off. Confident and untouchable. 'I'd asked him to find us a girl who could pass as a secretary, and he said she was the best typist he knew. He didn't say *why* she was so good.'

'Because she wanted to be a journalist.'

'Aye. Fuck's sake. He went and picked the one wee daft lassy who had big plans. And she stitched us up. Fucking Rab. She'd got a file. She was writing the whole damn story, taking pictures of us. Fucking joke.'

I stopped the tape and looked again through the files. The handwriting that I hadn't recognised now made sense as Jenny Towler's, building a file, showing the corruption, including documents from the council for planning permission and newspaper clippings of buildings that had burned down on the same site. The planning permissions in most cases predated the fire. The sort of thing people could get away with in the old days before everything was traceable.

But Jenny Towler had traced it.

My dad had traced it.

At the bottom of the pile of papers, and so on the outside of the bundle that I'd pulled out of the box, was a small handwritten note from my dad. It said that when the case was finally revealed, the newspaper should carry the byline of Jenny Towler.

I choked again, and this time I couldn't stop. I let the tears flow out and wiped at them uselessly with the sleeve of my jacket. Phil wrapped his huge arms around me, and I could feel tears on his chin. It wasn't what I needed. I couldn't get what I needed.

The front door rattled as someone tried the locked handle. Phil and Fran both turned towards the door, starting to move towards it, but Perera strode in the other direction. She headed towards the door that opened onto the hallway behind us, unclipping the holstered gun from her side.

'Get down,' she whispered to us as she passed. She switched the living room light off and then stepped into the hallway, moving on her toes towards the rooms at the back of the flat.

The front door rattled again, but this time we were following Perera's lead and seeing the bigger picture. I heard the sound of my bedroom window being forced open, and then a second later, loud and unmistakable in the confines of the flat, a gunshot.

Then the calm in the storm. For a second we were all still. Silence gripped the flat. Then we all started to move again. I felt sick, and I looked over at Phil, who was wiping his mouth, holding back a panic of his own. Perera then ran past us, through the living room and towards the front door. She almost ripped it off the hinges as she got it open and stepped out into the street. We heard her shout for someone to stop. Once, twice. The third time was followed straight away by two more gunshots, and then a sound of someone falling over and skidding across asphalt. Sirens could be heard in the distance, drawing near, along with the crackling of a police radio out in the street.

Perera stepped back in, not breaking a sweat, and looking like the coolest fucker on the planet.

'It's over,' she said.

Fifty-Three

I stood on a balcony overlooking Glasgow's city centre. In front of me was the glass pyramid roof of the St Enoch Centre, a shopping mall that had been expensively renovated to transform this part of the city. I leant over the frosted glass balcony to look down on the corner of Argyle Street and Buchanan Street, where high-street fashion met working-class budgets. It was the tail end of the rush hour, and all the sounds of the city mingled to float up at me. I'd lived in Glasgow my whole life without ever seeing it from this angle. Off to the right I could see the cranes of the dockyards, lit up at night to warn away low-flying pilots. To the left the balcony jutted out over the roof of the next building. If I leant over, I could make out the cathedral sitting atop the hill. I held out my mobile phone and marvelled at the full phone signal, which I never managed to get anywhere else in town, and then snapped off a few pictures of the view.

This was the life.

This could be my life.

Fiona Hunter stepped out onto the balcony with me. She was wearing a spotless combo of a shirt and cream slacks. She handed me a glass of red wine and nodded out at the night air, a gesture that somehow managed to take in the whole view.

'Well?' she asked. 'What do you say?'

'It's great.'

She sipped from her glass and looked out at the view as if she was seeing it for the first time. I watched her profile for a moment and wondered how hard she'd practised that look.

'I'm serious about the offer.' She turned to me. 'We own the flat below us as well. It could be yours—just come and work with us, full-time.'

'You guys must be seriously loaded.'

'We have good friends.' Douglas stepped out onto the balcony with us. He was dressed identically to Fiona. 'And good investment advice.'

I'd met Douglas briefly the night before, or more accurately the early hours of that morning, at the police station before the drive to my flat. After the shooting, we'd had another couple of hours of interviews and paperwork at the station, and then an attempt to piece together what had happened.

McLean and Gilbert had been wise to the fact it was a trap. They'd not shown up at Fran's office as planned, and Cummings had been ready to call off the operation when Perera had radioed in to say it was over. McLean had been the one rattling our door, a distraction that had worked on all of us except the cop. While we were supposed to be worrying about the front, Gilbert was coming in the back, where Perera ambushed him.

She'd then chased McLean down the street and, deciding she couldn't let an armed man run through Glasgow with his blood up, she fell back on her old training and put him down. Cummings told me in private she was going to be suspended until the top brass were satisfied she'd done the right thing, and that they were notoriously slow at deciding anything. I'd spent the night at Phil's, where he had a bedroom window that hadn't been forced open by a man with a gun. I didn't know how long it would be before I could feel safe in my own flat again, if ever. And around midday, when I finally convinced myself to get out of bed and face the world, Phil had asked if he could come with me next time I visited Dad. My phone started ringing soon after that, the same journalists who'd been calling me in the past about the insurance case, but now they were calling with huge offers of money, and the national media was pitching in. I ignored each one. It didn't feel like my story.

Some garbled version of the truth was starting to come out through the online outlets by mid-afternoon, and the radio had it too. None of them had it exactly right, but they all covered the broad strokes. They all cleared Mackie's name and talked about varying degrees of corruption and scandal. Some threw in sex, some threw in city councillors—everyone threw in the names McLean and Hillcoat.

The only source to get the story the way my dad had put it together in full was a small local paper: *The Clyde Evening News*. They'd been a paper I'd done work experience for when I was at school, and I still knew the editor. Nobody really read it any more, but back in the day, when a young woman named Jenny Towler had wanted to be a journalist, they'd been one of the city's biggest and finest papers.

They ran the story with her name on the byline.

There was one question that nobody seemed to be asking. One that only mattered if you needed to make sense of the whole thing, and it didn't look like anybody much cared about that. But I cared, and I needed to find the answer.

Towards the end of the working day I'd had a call from Fiona. She reminded me of the offer to go to her place for food and future, and I agreed to take her up on at least one of those things. I nursed one glass of red over a plate of souvlaki in their immaculate flat while they talked about how they'd met, what their plans were and how difficult it was to be taken seriously in the city. The flat was white and angular. Every surface was perfect, and every cushion and picture frame looked to be put in place using scientific instruments of precise measurement. Fiona started to get to the point by way of saying one of the other flats in the building was empty and that she could arrange for me to take a look at it if I was interested.

Out on the balcony, she handed me the second glass of wine and then tried again.

They stood on either side of me, leaning on the rails and sipping their wine. I couldn't figure either of them out as people, but I had a firm grasp on their businesses.

'Work for us,' Fiona said.

'You really impressed us yesterday,' Douglas said. 'Fiona was right about you. None of the older investigators in town would have done half of what you did.'

I aimed for the joke. 'They'd all have known better.'

'Maybe.' Fiona leant a little closer. 'Or maybe they've just let their ambition and interest slide with age. I'm told it happens to boring people. I don't think you'll ever find out.'

She actually said that.

'It doesn't have to be as an investigator,' Douglas said. 'We can find you other work. We're an emerging business. Plenty of opportunities for a project manager or a ridiculously overpaid assistant.'

They all sounded good. Too good. I already knew that. That was why I'd agreed to the dinner only, but standing on the balcony between them did turn my head for a moment, made me think about the offer.

Fiona brushed my hand with hers, almost casually, like it was an accident.

'If it helps,' Douglas said, 'we're flirting with you.'

'If it helps, I noticed.' I took my first sip from the wine and then laughed at my own joke. 'Did you flirt with Rab too? He was surely too old for you.'

Fiona swallowed her mouthful and watched me for a long, cold minute.

'When did you know?' she asked.

I shrugged off the question. 'When didn't I? The bullshit story Andy told me helped it along. Only a mug would believe all of this had been over a book deal. You hire me to find the guy at the centre of the whole conspiracy, the guy who started acting strangely and triggered this whole thing. The guy who ordered his own nephew killed. The way you took charge at the police station? Hell, even knowing I was there—that had to come through the wrong sources because I sure as hell didn't call you.'

'I'd hoped you would. That would have made things easier.'

'And then you orchestrate the whole thing. The shoot-out. You arrange for us to send the cops to Fran's place, you bully them into letting me go home and you set it up so that there will be an armed cop at the flat. Those phone calls you made at the police station? You called McLean, right? Told him that the meet at Fran's was a trap and that I was going home? I bet you failed to mention the armed cop.'

'Might have slipped my mind.'

'Ballsy move, calling them from the cop shop. Right in the lion's den.'

'I like ballsy moves.' She smiled at me. 'And *we* like you. You're only proving us right here. You're perfect. And I have to say, you're not the same person I met yesterday morning. You've woken up.'

I had.

'You went fishing for criminal contacts in Glasgow and found Rab because of his book deal.' I started to run through the story

I'd worked out. 'He started talking, telling you all about the property scams and the corrupt council, probably bigged himself up and made out like he was behind it all. And then, just when you were getting ready to talk money, his nephew started to figure out he'd been framed, and you told Rab the deal was off if he got found out.' I turned to Douglas. 'And you, Gomez Addams, what were you doing while all of this was going on?'

He mouthed *Gomez* at me with a question on his face while Fiona laughed.

'Never mind,' she said. 'You can get all the answers if you work for us. But you've got the important parts down. Well done. When we knew something had happened to Rab, we used you to smoke out the people we needed to talk to. But then you turned out to be a better investment than all of them put together. There's a lot to do, and the washer lady is looking to retire, hand her side of things over to someone else. Funnily enough, she seems to like you too.' She waved out at the view. 'This city. The Commonwealth Games and the referendum were just the start. There are people just waiting to come in here for a piece. Investors, builders, politicians. Everybody who is anybody will be making money off Glasgow for the next decade, and we're getting in on the ground floor. We'll be making money off their money.'

'Is this the same speech you gave to Rab? McLean? Gilbert?'

'A variation on it. But it's their own fault they got named in that recording, and that's changed things. Most of yesterday was about thinking on our feet. The plan kept changing.'

'You guys can't be paying for all of this alone.'

'You're perceptive. But you have to be all the way in before you get any more.'

This was all carrying the faintest whiff of Scientology. I wondered which level of the conspiracy I needed to be at before they told me about the giant lizards and taught me how to smile in a really suspicious way. Fiona brushed my hand again, and Douglas was in so close on my other side, I could feel his breath.

I pulled back and took a step towards the door.

'It would be a real shame if you said no.' Fiona pushed off from the railings and moved after me. 'A real waste of potential.'

'I don't think it would be the first time someone drank too much wine and fell from a balcony, though, in fairness,' Douglas said. I noticed how strong his muscles looked even in his skinny frame. 'Especially after such a stressful couple of days, nobody would blame you for finding it all too much.'

They both closed in on me.

I took another step back and felt the glass of the living room window behind me.

Fifty-Four

I've been rude,' I said. 'I feel bad about this. After you've gone to all this trouble and been such good hosts. I'm afraid I've used the same trick twice.'

I raised the phone that was still in my left hand. I turned the screen to face them so they could see the call was connected. There really was such a good phone signal up here. They both read the name *Cummings* at the same time. On cue the doorbell rang. Then the banging started, along with the other sound I'd come to get used to in the past couple of days, someone shouting, *'Police!'*

'You've set us up.' Fiona's perfect smooth face twisted into an animal snarl.

'No shit, Sherlock.'

The banging stopped, and I knew it was only seconds before the cops kicked in the door, but I decided to help them along. I shouted that we were here. Fiona punched me in the gut, really fucking hard, and I started to sink to my knees. In the end, that punch probably saved my life, because Douglas grabbed me by the shoulders of my shirt and tried to haul me over the balcony. If I'd been on my feet and on balance, he would probably have managed it. But I was a dead weight already sinking, and he didn't have the time to fight against that. He followed in with another punch in the same spot.

I watched from the floor as their feet ran away from me across the balcony. I raised my head to see the two of them climbing over the end and dropping out of sight. For a few moments I thought they'd jumped off the edge of the building, before I sucked in some air and sense and remembered that end of the balcony jutted out over the roof of the next building. The police swarmed out around me, and two of them helped me to my feet. I pointed over the end of the balcony and said the words *next* and *building* enough times for them to get the point.

Cummings stepped into my vision and asked if I was okay. I tried to answer that I was just peachy, but the punch had taken all of the sarcasm right out of me. He told me to head down and wait by the cars. I nodded and waddled over to the lift. On the way down I closed my eyes and controlled my breathing, just as I would after a difficult run, and got back in control.

It had been a good day, all told. I wasn't going to get the riches that Fiona and Douglas had been waving at me, and Hillcoat was dead, so I wouldn't be getting any further payments from him for solving the case. But I still had the advance he'd given me, and that added up to a thousand pounds. Not bad for two days' work. I still had Fran's divorce case to work on too, and that would lead to plenty of billable hours. I'd be fine until the end of the month, and by then, I hoped, all the media attention would have thrown some more work my way.

A crowd was gathering in the street, drawn by the police cars. The cops had parked at the junction between Argyle Street and Buchanan Street. Drunks from the nearby pubs had come to gawk and ask questions. I leant against the police car and started imagining a new office, with my name stencilled on the glass in the door.

A bottle of pear cider in the top drawer of my desk and a succession of attractive and scantily clad young men coming in through my door, looking for help.

Ireland Investigations.

That's who I was now.

I was going to make this work.

That's when I saw Fiona. She was skirting the edge of the crowd. I don't know how long she'd been there, or where her weird little helper had got to, but she was passing by ten feet from me. She'd found a dark hoodie from somewhere, and the cowl was covering her head, but I recognised her. She hadn't seen me, possibly blind-sided by the hood, but she was taking one last look up at the building. She turned to walk away and, as she did, she locked eyes with me. She kept walking, picking up the pace as she went. Soon she was trotting, and then running. She switched into a full sprint with a fluid motion. On instinct I started after her, breaking up through the gears faster than I should and not giving myself time to warm up. I remembered the previous morning and the anger I'd felt over her being a faster runner than me.

It was on.

She ran past Frasers and the Celtic shop, sidestepping early drunks and women with prams. She was pulling away from me even as I pushed myself. A car turned out of the bottom of Mitchell Street and Fiona had to pause, wait for it to move past and set off again around the back of it. I got within an arm's length, but again she started to put distance between us. At the junction with Jamaica Street, there was a whole load of people waiting at the pedestrian crossing. Fiona barged straight through them, in a mass of flailing arms and shouting, and jumped out into the traffic. She dodged a taxi and a double-decker bus. It looked like it had clipped her for a second as she sprawled forward onto the road, but it could have just been the wind as it passed her. While she climbed back to her feet, I had to wait for the bus to move on before I could give chase again. I ran out in front of another bus. The driver applied the brakes and the horn with equal anger, but I was out of the way before I could hear what he was shouting. The cars in the other two lanes had got the message by that point and slammed on the brakes, and I made it the rest of the way across.

Fiona had rounded the corner and headed beneath the Hielanman's Umbrella, the large glass-walled bridge that sat astride Argyle Street as an overpass for the trains. I heard them rumbling overhead. I went full-on Tom Cruise with the pumping fists as I ran, and got my head down. I was going to find the extra gear even if it killed me. Something clicked, that smooth feeling that takes over when you find the perfect running zone, and I started to gain on her. She must have felt me drawing close because she took a look back at me and then tripped over one of the beggars sitting in a shop doorway, and fell. The money from the upturned hat spread out across the pavement, and the beggar screamed out and started shouting in a language I didn't recognise, scrabbling around to pick up the coins. I grabbed Fiona by the hood and pulled her towards me, but she wriggled free and rolled away from me. She stood up and turned into the train station, started to run again as she found her balance. She headed down the escalator to the lower-level platforms, taking the moving steps two and three at a time, and I followed. She vaulted the ticket barrier before the guard could stop her, but it meant he'd had advance warning before I got there, and his arms were outstretched like a scarecrow's, blocking my path.

I took the direct option and barrelled right through him, knocking him over, and then climbed over the barrier. I'd apologise later, and I sent up a prayer to whoever was listening that he'd be okay about it once he understood.

Down the corridor and round the left-hand bend, and then down the old tiled steps onto the platform, I could hear Fiona's footsteps, but I was always just out of sight of her. On the platform I was closer than I thought, and I could almost reach out to grab her. The cramped space rumbled with an approaching train as it slowed to come into the station, and Fiona paused for a split second to look at it. In that moment I caught her, and we locked eyes, long enough for me to see she knew it, and long enough to feel like I'd achieved something. As I reached out to grab her, she twisted away from me, and her ankle buckled. She slipped, and as I made a second attempt to grab at her, she didn't help herself by trying to evade me again.

She fell forward, off the platform and into the path of the oncoming train.

I felt, rather than saw, the impact. The sound came a nanosecond later, the dull thudding of something heavy and meaty being sliced up by something heavier and metal. Then the screaming started, everyone on the platform reacting to what they'd just seen, and mingled with the high-pitched whine of the train's emergency brakes. I sank to my knees and thought, for just a moment, about how long it was going to be before I could eat meat again.

At some point later, maybe minutes, maybe hours, maybe decades, Cummings knelt down to smile at me. He helped me to my feet.

'Hey, Ireland,' he said. 'Who died and made you Batman?'

In spite of everything, I found a laugh. 'Don't mention that to my brother.'

'What?'

'Never mind.'

He stood up and offered a hand to pull me up, but I waved it away. I stood up under my own steam. I didn't need help. He was watching me, waiting to see what I did next.

'You okay?' he asked.

I smiled. 'I'm fine.'

Acknowledgements

Thanks to Al Guthrie for being the first person to challenge me to raise my game, back when I was starting out, and for being here now to bring this book across the line.

Thanks as always to Stacia Decker, who manages to put up with all my whining and yet still somehow thinks I'm worth representing. I get to be part of the coolest team in crime fiction.

Thanks to Emilie Marneur for bringing me across to the UK crew and for believing in this book, to Jill Pellarin for covering up my bad grammar, and Neil Hart for the right answer at the right moment.

Ray Banks and Jacque Ben-Zekry take turns keeping me in line. Johnny Shaw makes me want to bring a little more fun to the work. Erik Ben-Zekry kept me company late at night while I was working, and Christa Faust fed me a diet of some really shitty films at just the right time to get this whole project finished.

Thanks to all my family and friends in Glasgow, especially those who've managed to work their way into this book. Thanks to the city itself, for waking me up.

And, of course, thanks to my wife, Lisa-Marie, for every single thing.